Advance Praise for
A Long Way from Home

"Funny, fact-filled, and philosophical. This is an inspiring story for any kid who has been forced to move—to a new school, a new state, or a new point on the space-time continuum."

—Edward Bloor, author of *Tangerine* and *Taken*

"A blend of fantasy, science fiction, and coming-of-age, Laura Schaefer's smart middle-grade novel is *A Wrinkle in Time* for the modern day. From the first gripping page to the clever twist at the end, *A Long Way from Home* is sure to delight both avid and reluctant readers of all ages. You won't want to miss this remarkable book."

—Karen McQuestion, author of The Watchful Woods series

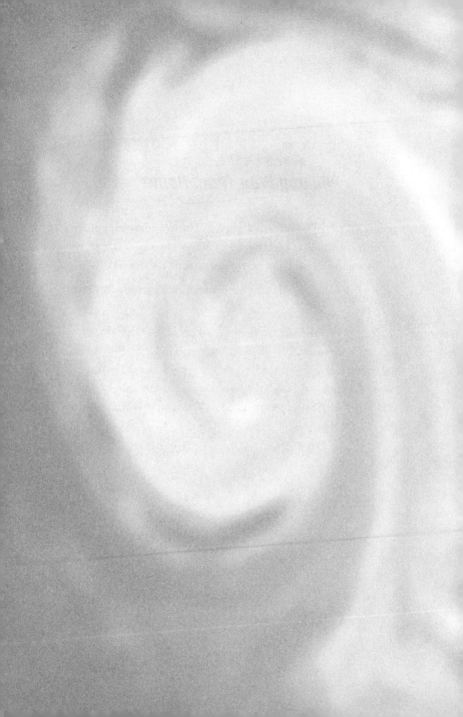

A Long Way from Home

Laura Schaefer

CAROLRHODA BOOKS
MINNEAPOLIS

Text copyright © 2022 by Laura Schaefer

All rights reserved. International copyright secured. No part of this book may be reproduced, stored in a retrieval system, or transmitted in any form or by any means—electronic, mechanical, photocopying, recording, or otherwise—without the prior written permission of Lerner Publishing Group, Inc., except for the inclusion of brief quotations in an acknowledged review.

Carolrhoda Books®
An imprint of Lerner Publishing Group, Inc.
241 First Avenue North
Minneapolis, MN 55401 USA

For reading levels and more information, look up this title at www.lernerbooks.com.

Jacket illustrations by Millie Liu.

Main body text set in Bembo Std.
Typeface provided by Monotype Typography.

Library of Congress Cataloging-in-Publication Data

Names: Schaefer, Laura, author.
Title: A long way from home / by Laura Schaefer.
Description: Minneapolis : Carolrhoda Books ®, 2022. | Audience: Ages 10–14. | Audience: Grades 4–6. | Summary: After moving with her family to Florida, twelve-year-old Abby is having a hard time coping, so when she meets two boys from the future she decides to escape the seemingly depressing present by traveling to their time with them.
Identifiers: LCCN 2021040420 (print) | LCCN 2021040421 (ebook) | ISBN 9781728416700 | ISBN 9781728460826 (ebook)
Subjects: CYAC: Time travel—Fiction. | Friendship—Fiction. | Anxiety—Fiction. | Family life—Fiction. | LCGFT: Novels.
Classification: LCC PZ7.S33232 Lo 2022 (print) | LCC PZ7.S33232 (ebook) | DDC [Fic]—dc23

LC record available at https://lccn.loc.gov/2021040420
LC ebook record available at https://lccn.loc.gov/2021040421

Manufactured in the United States of America
1-48922-49214-3/4/2022

For my mother, **Linda**,
and daughter, **Eleanor**.

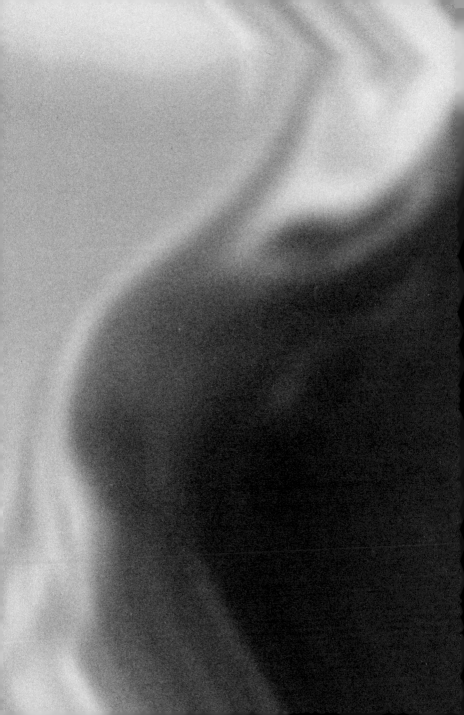

Do not look at stars as bright spots only.
Try to take in the vastness of the universe.

—Maria Mitchell, astronomer (1818–1889)

1

The summer I turn twelve, Mom and Dad finally let me have a phone. Dad buys me an old model, supposedly refurbished (I have my doubts), and the thing is glitchy right from the very beginning. Once in a while, I receive weird text messages from long streams of digits—longer than any regular phone number I've ever seen. They're not even messages, really. Just words. Single words that don't make any sense. But I don't delete them and I don't say anything about them to my parents, who are worried enough about me as it is.

The first word I receive is *HOUSE*. I stare at it for a while, confused. I text back, "You've got the wrong number," but the reply says, "Message failed to send."

1

This is what happens when your parents won't spring for a new phone, I think to myself.

I have more important things on my mind, though. Things that aggravate the knot in my stomach, which has its own unpredictable personality. Sometimes when Mom asks me about it, she does this thing with her eyes that makes my obsessive thinking seem like an extra member of our family. I've been to a few different doctors and psychologists, though none of them really help. They do try. It's their job to try.

But no therapist in the world can actually change any of the things that are making me worry, because they're big things—problems no one seems to know how to fix. No one can even agree on what the main problems *are*.

Things are just . . . not okay.

* * *

I find out we—Mom, Dad, me, and my cat, Jones—are moving because Mom got a new job. It isn't just any job, either. Mom's a physicist. A PhD. She's always saying she wants to do something *astonishing* and *significant* with her life. And she wants the same for me. That's why she's always bugging me to finish my math homework and "apply myself" because "the world needs my talents."

So now, she's going to work for this aerospace company that's trying to get humanity farther into space—faster and cheaper than has ever been done before, using a new kind of rocket called the Athena Heavy. The company, SpaceNow, has a big plan to strap twenty-seven of these rockets together and eventually get humans to Mars in something like comfort. The SpaceNow engineers are exceptionally good at applying themselves, so Mom wants to help them. And since my mother is an overachieving genius, she's been invited to do just that. Which means she won't be working from home anymore, like she's been doing most of my life, and we'll have to leave Pennsylvania for Florida—specifically Merritt Island, along the "Space Coast"—in the middle of my summer break.

I wonder if maybe the SpaceNow engineers and I have something important in common. We look around at Earth right now, at the burning rain forests and rising seas, and say: "Bring me my rocket, please. I have an 8:15 flight to Not Here."

* * *

I'm working on a theory. Mom is a scientist who is always using theories, so why shouldn't I? My theory is we are, all of us, right now, living in a dystopia. Sure, our dystopia is maybe a teeny less obvious than the ones in some stories. But think about it—do the people in the backgrounds of the books and movies even *realize* they're living in a place that is *off*? A few of them, sure. But not most.

There's a constant, low-key dread in the air. It feels like the world is holding its breath, as if the bottom could fall out at any moment, as if something important is permanently broken. My best friend, Olivia, is trying to talk her parents into letting her be homeschooled from now on. She says she feels safer when she doesn't have to leave the house too much. She says she's happiest in her room.

Think about the Great Pacific Garbage Patch.

It's this enormous churn of plastic and other trash floating in the ocean between California and Hawaii. The whole disaster is in international waters, so no government is doing anything much about it. The Patch is twice the size of the state of Texas and very difficult to clean up because some of its particles— the ones getting eaten by sea life—are extremely small. There are something like 1.6 trillion pieces of plastic out there, swirling, swirling, swirling around in the waves. The Great Pacific Garbage Patch isn't unique either. It's just the biggest of five.

Imagine you're a fish who usually lives deep in the ocean. You swim toward the light above for a nice big meal. You power yourself through the water toward the promise of the sun, and some delicious-looking morsel catches your eyeball. You swim and swim, straining to reach the light—and that yummy morsel. You gulp it right down. But it's not food. It's a broken plastic container.

Or, forget about the fish. It's not like humans don't have our own problems. Think about the glaciers you'll never get to see. Think about floods and power grid failures. Are you an animal lover? Sorry to hear that, since hundreds of species of animals are about to disappear forever.

Dystopia.

Last semester, one of my teachers—Mr. Arnold, who teaches sixth-grade concert band—did kind of help me when my stomach knot was getting a lot worse after the latest mass shooting. I talked to him sometimes in my clarinet lesson during flex hour. I explained my dystopia theory, and his eyes crinkled up like he was about to laugh. Then he coughed and apologized and said he could definitely see my point.

Mr. Arnold didn't talk about my obsessive worrying like it was some huge deal. He said he felt concerned a lot, too, about the state of the world—and that the only thing that ever helped his anxiety was when he *did* something.

He encouraged me to fix one tiny problem I worried about. Mr. Arnold said this was all we could do, and that if everyone on Earth worked on one problem, we'd all be just fine. Probably.

And if not, I should practice my instrument anyway because we had a concert coming up.

* * *

Toward the end of the school year, I researched and wrote a feature for my school paper about plastic and why it's so bad for the ocean. We only use most plastic items once and throw them out—but a lot of things like bags and water bottles and stuff are never recycled. They pollute the Earth for years and years. I spent a long time on that article, even though no one told me to.

Everyone liked my story. Olivia said she would never touch a plastic bag or plastic water bottle again for as long as she lived. She was already using a metal water bottle, but I appreciated what she said anyway.

Mom lost her mind, telling practically everyone she knew about the article. She kept saying, "See, Abby? Doesn't it feel great to do something positive?!"

It was super annoying. I could make a whole list of Mom's YOU CAN DO IT sayings, but I'd rather not because I hear them more or less constantly. My mother looks like a gymnast, like a small bundle of muscle and energy, with her hair kept short because it's more efficient that way. I'm completely different, long-limbed and awkward, with dark, thick, long hair that always clogs the shower drain.

Anyway, after I wrote that article, every time I saw a piece of plastic trash outside, I stopped and picked it up so it wouldn't find its way to the ocean. Picking up garbage kind of became my hobby. It felt good—until I googled, *What actually happens to our recycling?*

Some questions have not-great answers, which is why being able to ask them anywhere, anytime, isn't always the best.

* * *

Mom is an optimist who believes the future will get better, that the present moment and all of its issues can be solved for. My knotted-up stomach and I are not so sure.

Have you ever scrolled through your phone for a few minutes, then climbed into the narrow space between your bed and the wall, covered yourself up with a comforter, and wished you could escape?

I have.

2

T-MINUS 33 DAYS TO LAUNCH

One night, three days before we leave, I can't eat. I've just said goodbye to Olivia. I know I will have zero friends once we move. Mainly because I don't plan on making any. I look around our boxed-up living room and chew on my bottom lip. *Goodbye, carpet stain shaped like New Jersey. Goodbye, curtains sewn by Grandma. Goodbye, super-loud creak in the kitchen floor.*

"Can't you move by yourself?" I mumble to Mom, who is packing up the kitchen. "I'll visit you on weekends. Just because *you* have to move to Florida to save the world doesn't mean we all do."

I've been to Merritt Island a few times on family trips, because Mom's obsessed with the Kennedy Space Center. All I really remember about the place

9

is that it's hot and the air is heavy and the storms are apocalyptic.

"We're a family, Abigail. I'm so sorry, I really am. I know this isn't easy, what I've asked you to do, but I need you to be strong and make the best of it."

I think about the tree outside my bedroom window, how I track its changes as the seasons go by, how I'll miss its steady and predictable cycle. I think about this croissant Dad sometimes gets for me at a bakery we can ride our bikes to . . . how it crackles when I bite into it and rains flaky dough down onto the table. I think about the tennis court down the block, the shop where we buy reeds for my clarinet, the friendly librarian at our school's media center, all my classmates I've known forever. I feel a lump in my throat and try to swallow. "I don't want to go."

"You'll survive," Mom says, from the pantry. "Focus on the positives."

"I can't."

I hear her sigh. Mom has a long record of not being a fan of my attitude. "Go pack up your bathroom drawers. It can't wait anymore."

* * *

I have a great-aunt who was once in the space business, like Mom. Only it wasn't a business when she was in it—it was more like a national pastime, part of what made being an American special. Nora Carlyle. You can google her. You'll find some stuff—like the fact that she lives on Merritt Island, not far from the house Mom and Dad just bought. But you won't find the answer to the question I really want to ask, which is *Why does Mom hate you?*

Nora, like my mother, is a certified genius. She's some kind of an engineering mastermind who once did a lot of important stuff for NASA, but it's her reputation as a scary recluse that has me interested. I guess the more sensitive way to put it is she has agoraphobia, a fear of leaving her house. So she doesn't. And she hasn't for years.

Mom and Nora were close, once upon a time, but now they're estranged. Which means *not speaking.* I looked it up. Mom won't talk about it with me because she "chooses not to dwell on the negative." Neither will Dad, although he did tell me that he and Mom tried to visit Nora's house years ago, during one of our vacations to Merritt Island when I was really little, and she reminded him of Miss Havisham from *Great Expectations*, a super long book written about a thousand years ago by Charles Dickens. I just started to read it. It's pretty good.

I wonder if Nora knows that we'll be moving so close to her—within easy walking distance, if my online sleuthing is accurate. I wonder if she would care if she did know.

* * *

Later that night, I stare at the ceiling. It's after eleven, and there's nothing else in my room right now besides me, an air mattress, and my old glow-in-the-dark stars on the wall. They don't glow anymore, but I can reach for them from memory—they're arranged not in a constellation, but in the shape of a heart because I was only five when I put them up. Lying on my side, I pick at one small star with the edge of my fingernail. It won't budge.

Even though they're just stickers that I haven't touched or even thought about in years, it makes me sad I have to leave them behind here, in their forlorn heart formation. They're a piece of my history, a happy piece.

I can't sleep, so I go to my YouTube app. I ask the search bar some version of what I always ask when I'm feeling particularly anxious: *Are we going to be okay?*

A list of musicians, news-types, and a few TED talk people tell me we will be.

I eventually fall asleep.

3

T-MINUS 30 DAYS TO LAUNCH

During the first leg of our drive to Florida, Mom is in a chatty mood. I try to leave my earbuds in and ignore her, but she keeps telling Dad and me (and Jones, who's meowing mournfully in his cat carrier) trivia about SpaceNow. She's full of nervous, excited energy.

"Did you know that SpaceNow failed its first three launch attempts?" Mom says, turning around in the front passenger seat to face me.

"No," I say, removing one bud with a sigh. "That was before I was born."

"Now you're making me feel old," Dad laughs. He catches my eye in the rearview mirror and winks.

"You *are* old," I say, smiling at him.

"No, he's not!" Mom protests. "Besides, age is just a number."

I roll my eyes. *Age is just a number* until I decide I want to try driving the car or get my eyebrow pierced. Mom can be so oblivious to reality beyond, like, neutrinos.

I look out the window as she keeps talking. "SpaceNow started with a dream: to land a packet of gel on Mars, to grow plants in its soil."

"And how's that project going?" I ask. I'm being a jerk, because I already know SpaceNow isn't actively doing anything on Mars. It's simply too hard to get to and from our closest planetary neighbor regularly, even though SpaceNow is now a $30 billion company employing more than five thousand people.

"It's *not* going, at the moment," Mom admits. "But it will. We have a significant, history-making launch coming up in T-minus thirty days. And a dream is what started it all. Isn't that amazing? We should talk more about dreams. They're powerful."

"So, when are we moving to Mars, then?"

Mom ignores the question and instead launches into a little speech about how colonizing Mars is definitely going to happen, and how great that will be, because sending a bunch of overachievers to another planet will get us all "thinking big." I'm not so sure about this. Who, precisely, are the people who will get to go? Are they all going to be millionaires and billionaires or working for one of them? Who *won't* get to go? Who gets to decide?

"I don't know, Mom," I say. "What if climate change kills us all first?"

"Climate change on Earth is no joke," Mom says, her voice turning somber for once. "But it doesn't mean we can all just sit around and do nothing and blame each other for it like a bunch of fighting toddlers. This push into space will lead to breakthroughs that will help all of humanity. That's what I choose to believe."

I sigh. My stomach begins hurting, and we don't have a bathroom break scheduled for at least another two hours.

"You know what's interesting, though?" she goes on. "The things human beings have done on Earth that are so terrible—causing climate change by burning through all our fossil fuels and developing the nuclear bomb—will be *the very same things* that help us transform Mars into a habitable place."

"Uh, what?" I pull out my second earbud and look at her again.

"See, what we'll do once we get there, eventually—soon!—is pump methane into Mars' atmosphere and explode bombs on the poles to warm the place up. Melting ice from the explosions will release carbon dioxide into the atmosphere. This will heat the planet to more comfortable, near-Earth temperatures and start an active water cycle of weather. We need to create an atmosphere that protects humans from radiation, and this will do it. Then we'll have to start pumping in oxygen to make Mars's air breathable. So, yes, we've made some mistakes here on Earth, but we've learned so much, and we can take that knowledge with us. In other words, it's all in how you look at things!"

"Mom, come on. What will stop people from ruining Mars too? Maybe we should fix things here before we go around messing up the entire solar system."

"I think we can do both."

"See! You admit we'll mess it up."

"I'm not . . . no, that's not what I was trying to say. I think we can improve the way we do things here *and* explore the neighborhood."

I snort. *The neighborhood.* "I'm going to try to nap now."

"Fine, Grumpy McGrumperson. Dad and I will go to Mars without you." Mom turns back around in her seat, giving up on me for the time being.

"Did you say the air there is going to smell like methane?" Dad asks.

"Maybe a little," Mom admits. "Don't worry about it."

4

Our new house on Merritt Island feels more like a rented condo than a place I'm supposed to call home. The walls are all white and instead of carpet on the floor, there's tile. The ceilings are very high.

"I got you the lavender shower gel you like!" Mom says, returning from an epic Target run. "See, some things won't change."

"Thanks," I say. "New shower gel definitely makes up for everything."

"Right?" Mom is extra chipper and smiley. "Isn't it amazing how big the bathrooms are here?"

"Not really," I say. "I liked our old bathroom."

"Abby, you know it's been scientifically proven that moods are contagious. Let me infect you with my enthusiasm."

"I'm sad," I say. "Let me be sad."

Mom sighs and returns to unpacking her Target haul. Dad is visiting local marinas, looking for a place that's not too far away from our house to keep his small boat. The only reason he agreed to this move to Florida, I think, is that he'll be able to go fishing a lot more often here.

After Mom shuts herself in her home office to get some work done, I sneak over to my great-aunt's property, which is only a few blocks away. I feel like I should warn Nora that Tropical Cyclone Dr. Anna Monroe (aka Mom) has just arrived, practically on her doorstep. Maybe we can form an alliance to deal with her.

My great-aunt's house is surrounded by a painted cinderblock wall that's overgrown with flowering vines. A small sign says BEWARE OF DOG. The house behind it is big and Spanish-style. I can't see much of it—only glimpses through the gaps between the outer wall and the front gate. But what I can see looks awesome. There are fountains and cobblestones and climbing vines. If I lived here, I'd never leave either.

When I ring the bell at the gate, there's no response.

***

Starting seventh grade here is weird. For one thing, the school is brand new, just like the house my parents chose for us. You might think this would be a good thing, but everything is too white, too clean, too prison-like. The floors are polished concrete, and the air conditioning is set to *stun*. On the whiteboard, my homeroom teacher has written COLD IS BETTER THAN MOLD in big block letters. I think she's probably trying to convince herself. The main building is surrounded on three sides by rows of these connected trailers called "portables" to handle the overflow of students.

This school has three times as many kids as my old school up north because, as Dad says, "Everyone and their brother is moving to Florida right now," and it feels like barely controlled chaos, especially at lunch. It's confusing and loud and cold, and I don't like being here at all. I don't understand why I can't go to a small private school like I did back home. Mom made all these noises about my new school being "A-rated" and "STEM-focused," but I wonder if she knew about all the portables when she and Dad were enrolling me. Not to mention the barely contained mold problem.

OLIVIA: How was your first week? I miss you!

ABBY: *crying face emoji* I miss you too.

OLIVIA: I want to quit band but my parents say I can't.

ABBY: Why?

OLIVIA: Because my flute cost four thousand dollars.

ABBY: No, why do you want to quit?

OLIVIA: Mr. Arnold is making me play first chair.

ABBY: Oh.

I feel a stab of jealousy. *I* want to play first chair in band. But not here—back home, where I understand what that would be like. Back home, where my teacher really knew me and what I could do. Here, my clarinet stays in my closet; I've told Mom and Dad I want to spend my first semester of seventh grade getting used to things before doing anything extra.

The truth is, I don't want to find out where I'd stand in a band with a hundred and fifty kids in it. That's too many. Back home we had twenty-eight.

Mom doesn't notice when I only give her one-word answers to her questions. Or maybe she does notice, but she doesn't say anything about it. Her new job is overwhelming. Twelve-hour days during our first week living here have quickly become fifteen hours long, sometimes more, not counting the extra work she puts in on Saturdays. She seems happy, though, saying the Athena Heavy launch at the end of August is going to make history.

Dad is also giving me space because he's busy arguing with contractors and learning how to grout tile. The downstairs bathroom isn't finished yet, so he's trying to tackle the job himself. He likes Florida and wants me to get excited about it. He gives me a tear-off calendar that features a different attraction for each day of the year.

Today's is Solomon's Castle, a place some guy built himself in the middle of nowhere and covered with aluminum foil.

Perfect.

5

Chocolate shakes make me feel a little better, so I walk to a Checkers after school. It's a million degrees in Florida in late August. Walking anywhere outside is miserable, but it's worth it for a shake. Along the way, I google *At what temperature does the human body spontaneously combust?* Answer: three thousand degrees.

Right as I step up to the counter to order, I notice this boy here too. He's my age, and he looks confused, as if he can't quite figure out the procedure for ordering food. His pants, shirt, and even his shoes are all made of the same extremely weird-looking material. His clothing appears to be soft and is all one shade of light gray. The boy has his sleeves pushed up his tan arms, and his dark brown hair is wild—shaved on

24

one third of his head and longish and wavy on the rest. A younger boy is with him.

Even though I like the unusual look of this kid, it isn't like me to talk to people I don't know, so I step up to the counter to order and decide to ignore him.

That's when the boy starts pressing on the soda dispensers even though he doesn't have a cup to catch the liquid. When soda pours out of the machine at his touch, he jumps back, shocked. Somehow, I just know that he isn't trying to make trouble. Neither the boy nor his younger brother (friend?) are laughing.

When the lady at the counter says, "Hey!" the boy immediately begins apologizing. But I can tell the lady is on the verge of kicking them out.

"Do you need some help?" I ask. My cheeks turn warm. "I mean, I can tell you what's good if you've never been to a Checkers before."

The boy smiles at me. His smile is nice and his brown eyes look friendly.

The younger boy at his side has yellow hair clipped close to his head. He watches me intently but doesn't make direct eye contact; it feels like he is staring at a space just behind my head. He also doesn't smile. I notice that even though the two are both out of place, they hold themselves with confidence, almost as if nothing they see impresses them. But then again, why would it? There's nothing particularly impressive about a fast-food restaurant.

"Thank you," the first boy says, his voice deeper than I expect it to be. Maybe he's a smidge older than I'd thought. "I never have. But I don't have any money."

"Oh," I say, wondering why they're in here, then. "I could, um, buy you a shake? Or are you waiting for someone?"

"I don't know what that is, but sure. Thank you. We're not waiting for anyone."

"You don't know what a shake is?" What is with this kid? He may be cute, but there is a good chance he needs more help than I can give him. I order three small chocolate shakes.

"I do not." He smiles again. I swallow and pay for our order using my allowance. These two are lucky I recently got a *my-parents-feel-guilty* raise. "We're a long way from home."

6

"I'm a long way from home too," I reply. At least the place *I'm* from has chocolate shakes. "Are you on vacation?" I ask. It isn't the regular time of year to be on a family trip, but who knows how school calendars work in Canada? Or wherever the boy and his little brother are from.

"Not exactly," he says. "My name is Adam. This is Bix. What's yours?"

"Abby. Nice to meet you." We all three shake hands, which feels strange and formal, but Adam started it. His hand feels nice in mine. Strong and not sweaty.

"Nice to meet you too. So, this is Earth? I love it." He looks around the not-particularly-clean restaurant and his eyes land on the window. It's hazy outside, the hottest part of the day.

"Um . . . yes. The last time I checked. Are you okay?"

Our shakes appear at the counter, and I hand one each to Adam and Bix, who both watch me take a sip. They copy my actions, and their eyes light up as I lead them to a booth.

"I'm smooth. This is delicious!" Adam says, sliding into a seat across from me. Bix moves in next to him.

"Very gratifying," Bix agrees, sounding much more sophisticated than your average fourth grader. "There must be an extremely elevated amount of sugar in this beverage."

"Uh, yeah," I say. "There is. It's made of ice cream, you know? I can't believe you've never been in a Checkers before. I figured they had these everywhere."

"Nope, not everywhere. *I* can't believe I'm trying ice cream and meeting the nicest girl in the galaxy on the same day," Adam says, grinning. "Things are turning out to be better than I expected on this vector. Thank you, Abby."

I choke on my shake and manage to recover without spewing it all over the table (it's close). "You're welcome." I'm mystified. I don't know what to say. *Vector?*

"We've come from a long distance away, and we need some help. My sister is lost somewhere nearby, and we don't know where," Adam explains, pushing the long side of his hair back from his eyes. "We need to find her as soon as possible. She may be sick."

"Oh no!" I say. "That's so scary. Have you called the police?"

"We'd . . . rather not do that," Bix says. His eyes are intense, as if he's looking right through me. He pulls out a tablet with an oval screen and starts typing on it, shaking his head as if he can't quite get it to do what he wants it to.

I stare at the unusual screen shape and try to remember if I've ever seen anything like it before. I don't think so.

"At least the solar noon is past. The temperature outside should begin to decline soon." Bix says this to Adam, ignoring me. Adam gives him a curt nod.

"What about your parents?" I ask.

"We need to find V—her name is actually Vanessa, but she hates it—before our parents realize we aren't on our ship," Adam says. "Or she'll get in big trouble."

"Okay . . ." I say. I understand that the police can cause problems for people who are from a "long distance" away, and when Adam says "ship," I picture one of the enormous cruise ships currently docked at Port Canaveral a couple miles away. I want to help. Somehow, Adam feels familiar to me. "What do you need?"

"We have some equipment that can help us locate V," Adam says, gesturing to the oval tablet Bix is frowning at. "But it's going to take some time, so . . ."

"We need a place to sleep," Bix finishes for him. "This restaurant will not suffice and we may be here for days."

I stare at them both, overwhelmed and unsure of what to say. I kind of want to text Mom, problem-solver extraordinaire, but something stops me. A solution pops into my head. "How do you feel about small boats?" I ask. "Like, real small?"

"Love them," Adam says.

* * *

I lead Adam and Bix toward the marina where Dad is storing his boat. I figure they can sleep onboard for the night, because at the moment Dad is too busy getting our house habitable to worry about exploring the island channels with his rod and reel.

The afternoon sun is merciless. I'm glad I have my sunglasses, which I hope look at least a little bit cool. At my old school, I never worried that much about what I looked like. Back home, everyone in my class felt like my sibling because we'd been together since kindergarten. But here, I think about it a lot. No one knows me, so to them I'm just a collection of boring clothing, painfully skinny limbs, and long hair. I try to put it out of my mind and focus on the present moment, a technique one of my many therapists used to always harp on.

I shade my eyes and observe Adam and Bix, who both tilt their faces *toward* the sun.

"Aren't you worried about getting a sunburn?" I ask them. Dad is always following me around with spray sunscreen.

"Negative," Bix says. "The UV index today is a seven, which means we have at least fifteen to twenty minutes before the sun has any adverse effects. Also, Vitamin D3 is being made in our skin thanks to this sun exposure. It's photolysis of 7-dehydrocholesterol in the epidermis."

"Oh," I say. "Okay."

"Aren't you glad you asked?" Adam says, grinning at me. "You'll have to excuse Bix here. He's very . . ."

"Don't worry about it," I interrupt with a wave of my hand. "I have a family member who's the same way, if you get her going on the right topic."

Adam looks relieved. "You're easy to talk to, Abby."

"Thanks." I smile at him and shift my backpack to the other shoulder. It's clear plastic, which means it's ridiculous, uncomfortable, *and* environmentally unfriendly. Right before we moved, Dad read some article that said backpacks in Florida schools had to be clear, so he bought me one even though this was no longer a thing and had never even *been* a thing in our particular county. But when I told him this, he said, "It's perfectly good for now; we'll get you a new bag when it wears out." I thought about lobbying Mom for something cute, but I decided to wait and get my own instead. She'd definitely bring one home from work featuring a giant SpaceNow logo, and that's not the look I'm going for.

"It's so beautiful here," Adam says, taking a deep breath. "Completely icy. I love all the cars! It must feel amazing to drive one of them."

"Um, probably . . ." I say. I've never thought about it before. And . . . *Icy?* Not even close. Stifling. Boiling. Roasting. "Are there more cars here than you're, uh, used to seeing?"

"You could say that," Bix says. Something in his tone makes me reluctant to demand to know where they're from.

We're walking on a pretty busy commercial street. Nothing about it is special in my eyes. There are a lot of cars, but since when is that a good thing? Dad is one of the most good-natured people in the whole world, and even he thinks Florida drivers are the worst. He says that when someone cuts him off in traffic, he tries to imagine them as a giant, over-enthusiastic golden retriever, because it's impossible to stay mad at a golden retriever.

Adam sniffs. "I can smell salt in the air."

I breathe deeply like he is doing and notice a trace of the ocean. "You're right. We're pretty close to the beach here. It's just over one more bridge."

"I've *got* to see it," Adam says. "I've never been to a beach."

"I haven't actually seen it yet myself," I admit. "My family just moved here a few weeks ago. I'm still getting adjusted." I casually play off my churning stomach, happy I sound somewhat normal instead of like the walking anxiety attack that I actually am.

"We should go together!" Adam says. "As soon

as possible! Tomorrow."

"It's a date," I agree immediately. "I mean, uh, not a date . . . just, you know, a plan. Something we should do."

"For sure," Adam says. "Tremendous!"

Bix sighs. "There's no clock for shenanigans."

We finally reach the marina's deserted front gate. I type in the code I'd seen Dad use and show the boys the boat. Its cabin is small and a little musty-smelling, but not too bad. There are built-in seats with cushions and a kitchen area with a bolted-down table and tiny cupboards. I know the fridge is mostly empty, but I do find sodas and pretzels.

"Is there anything else I can get for you guys?" I ask, handing over the snacks. "Toothbrushes?"

Adam shakes his head and smiles. "This is perfect, Abby. Thank you."

My phone buzzes. It's another word from the long string of numbers. Actually, it's not a word. This time, it's a name: *STUART.* I ignore it.

7

Have you ever gotten an idea out of nowhere, fully formed? I have. Mom says it's because I'm just as smart as she is. (I'm not sure if that's true, or if she just *wants* it to be true.) Sometimes she'll talk about physics with me. She gets a twinkle in her eye, and you can tell that considering the mysteries of the universe is the thing that makes her feel most alive.

There's this thing she told me about a while ago that I think about sometimes.

It's called the causal loop paradox. Here's how it works: imagine a time traveler copies a mathematical proof from a textbook, or maybe a set of song lyrics if you want to be less nerdy about it. Then, the time traveler goes back in time to meet the mathematician or the songwriter who first wrote the proof or the song, before any writing has actually happened.

The time traveler allows the mathematician to simply copy the proof, or maybe gives the songwriter the new song, like, telepathically. Mom told me that's how Paul McCartney wrote "Yesterday." The whole song appeared in his head, in a dream. It was so good Paul was totally freaked out that he had subconsciously stolen someone else's work. He even thought of the song as some kind of lost-and-found item and said he figured that if no one claimed it after a few weeks, he could have it.

Anyway, just like that, the information in the math proof has no origin, and the song arrives as if from thin air.

Here's what I can't stop thinking about: *What if everything we ever do is like that?* Maybe our future selves are always visiting us, nonstop, giving us ideas that we trick ourselves into believing are thoughts we invented. I'd like to talk to my future self. Ask for her help. I wonder what she would tell me, if she could.

Physics is a lot of math. But it's also a little bit fascinating, if you ask the right questions.

* * *

Back at the house, where Dad is still locked in single combat with the downstairs bathroom, I sit in my bedroom with my phone, reading about the people who are trying to get into the United States from other countries. Meeting Adam and Bix is making me worried about what could happen if someone discovers them hiding out in Dad's boat. Will they be arrested?

Will *I* be arrested for helping them?

Even the families asking for asylum in our country are being held in detention centers. I read about children who made the journey alone, still waiting to be reunited with family members. Some never will be. I've mentioned this to my parents a few times, but they don't have the answers any more than I do. And they don't want to make my anxiety worse, so we don't talk much about the news.

The problem is that avoiding something like that doesn't make it go away.

Dystopia.

***

I need to stop scrolling, so I pull out a folder that I keep hidden in my desk.

Nora used to write my mother long emails. Mom saved some of them in a file on our family computer that I discovered when I was still in fifth grade. I printed the letters out, and I look at them sometimes. They're about college and work mostly, things I know nothing about. I think they were written a long time ago, as in twenty years ago, and I don't have Mom's part of the conversation, so it's confusing. But I've kept them.

I reread the first one I found:

Dear Anna,

You have to understand it was a lot different then. When I went to college, I was one of four women who graduated in a class of 250 mechanical engineers. When you're in such a small minority, you're extra conscious of the impressions you make.

I can tell you not to do that to yourself, but you probably will anyway. You feel like you HAVE to prove that you belong there. You get anxiety over failure no matter how many people like me tell you to relax. I was never able to relax. Am never able to now.

So, I get what you wrote about last week, even as I wish for better for you.

I remember feeling like, if a person asks a question and a lot of people have that same question, your classmates are thankful that you asked. But if a you ask something that turns out to be a simple, basic, "stupid" question, now you've wasted everyone's time and lose respect.

Whenever I asked the wrong question, I felt like I was confirming the belief that women shouldn't pursue this career path.

Many of these feelings were self-imposed, of course, but were based on experiences of being belittled from a young age just for being myself. Guys, it always seemed, could fail and just retake the class. If girls failed, they usually switched majors.

I internalized failure. "It's my fault," I would be the first to say. "I cost my team money. I should've been a better engineer. I'm not smart enough. I'm not good enough."

Don't do this to yourself. You ARE smart enough.

I'm sure none of this helps much. But I'm always here to talk.

~N

8

T-minus 6 days to launch

The next morning in homeroom, I take a seat as far from the front of the classroom as possible. I avoid eye contact with everyone, shiver as usual in the ridiculous air conditioning, and text Olivia.

ABBY: I met a boy.

OLIVIA: WUT. Tell me everything

ABBY: He's nice. He doesn't go to my school.

OLIVIA: Pic?

ABBY: I didn't get one.

OLIVIA: I'll wait. Name?

ABBY: Adam

There's a kid two desks over from me with a rubber band around his whole head, which secures a pink rectangular eraser to a spot just above his eyebrows. I watch as he takes the spring out of one of his pens and twists it into the eraser, then hooks the protruding half of the spring around one tooth of a comb he pulls out of his bag. The whole thing flops around his head. No one pays attention to him at all, as if this is just normal Floridian behavior. Which it probably is. Moving here is scarring me forever, no doubt.

I text Mom.

ABBY: My teacher says we have to take the FCAT standardized tests every single day until we are old enough to drive, and for a few years after that just to be sure.

MOM: Funny. Look on the bright side, you'll get extra good at tests! National Merit Scholarship, here we come!

ABBY: ☹

Another message pops up on my phone.

957300001111188856777000000000334545422: ANASTASIA

ABBY: Who is this? Who is Anastasia? [message failed to send]

"Abby? Abby Monroe?" I don't know how many times my homeroom teacher, Miss Bascom, says my name, but it's probably at least four. It's difficult to figure out the meaning of texts from a mysterious number sending you words and names you don't understand *and* pay attention to moment-to-moment reality at the same time.

"Yes?"

"Phone."

Busted.

"But I need it," I say. I briefly consider showing my teacher the strange message I'd just received but decide against it. House. Stuart. Anastasia. What does it mean?

"Mmmhmm," Miss Bascom says. "Hand it over. You can have it back at lunch. I'll give it to the guidance counselor after the language arts block."

ABBY: On hiatus until further notice. Equipment confiscated. Send help.

MOM: Good. Pay attention in class, maybe you'll learn something. I have a good feeling about this school.

ABBY: I have a bad feeling about it.

MOM: Apply yourself.

* * *

Mom and Dad are worried about the effect of our move on my psyche (AS THEY SHOULD BE), so I have to see the guidance counselor at my school before lunch. Mr. Hernandez has a decent enough face and a tie with cartoon characters on it. His desk is a disaster, which makes me kind of like him. Just for being different than Mom.

"Abby, your mother gave me a call. I hope you don't mind."

"I guess not," I say. I wonder what he'd say if I did mind. I look at my shoelaces and pick at the skin around my fingernails like I always do when I get nervous.

"I want you to make friends and feel comfortable here at JFK Middle School. Your parents and I discussed it, and we think you'd be an excellent candidate for our Where Everyone Belongs program."

"Um, your what?" I look at Mr. Hernandez in horror. I'm suspicious of any kind of program, especially one with the word "belong" in it.

"It's a terrific mentorship program for new students here," he explains. "We pair up sixth graders with mentors in seventh or eighth grade so they have an immediate buddy—someone to help them navigate our school."

"But I'm a seventh grader," I remind him.

"I know. But it's for all students who are new to our community. You'll like your mentor. Her name is Juliana and she's very friendly. She is one of our very best WEB mentors. She'll help make your transition smooth and fun."

"I really appreciate it, Mr. Hernandez, but I'd rather not."

He laughs. "Give it a week. As a personal favor to me."

I sigh and nod. I hate it how adults always act like you have a choice in the matter when they make a suggestion. If there's no way I'm getting out of something, I'd rather just hear "This is how it is. Deal with it."

Mr. Hernandez explains that I should meet Juliana at Table 14 in the cafeteria for lunch. At least he hands over my phone, with the warning that I am not to use it in class.

I go to my locker, grab the insulated lunch bag Dad packed for me, and trudge to my assigned table. So much for hiding out in the media center in front of a computer like I had planned.

"You must be Abby Monroe!" A petite girl sits down about a foot closer to me than I would prefer. Her black hair is in a braid. She has a dimple in each of her cheeks that makes her look like an actor you'd see on the Disney Channel. "I'm Juliana, your Where Everyone Belongs mentor!"

"Um, hi," I say, scooting away from her.

"Don't you just love JFK so far?"

"Yeah, it's okay," I say. I unpack my lunch sack and see that Dad followed my instructions and made me a Nutella sandwich on white bread. At least one thing is going my way. I take a photo of it with my phone and send it to Olivia. She replies with a snap of her burrito. I feel a little bit less alone. I picture the cozy little lunch room at my old school and wish I could transport myself there.

"As part of the Where Everyone Belongs program," Juliana persists, knocking me out of my daydream, "it's my job to get to know you, so I've prepared a list of questions to ask. Are you ready?"

"I guess so." I nibble at my sandwich and look at her.

"What do you want to be when you grow up?"

"I don't really know yet," I admit. "I'm not sure we *will* grow up. Maybe a journalist."

Juliana looks at me, blinks, and decides to ignore the first part of my comment. "I want to work on a cruise ship. Or be a veterinarian. Or maybe be a veterinarian *on* a cruise ship."

"Is it okay if we do more mentoring later?" I ask. "I need to visit the media center."

"Sure! I'll come with you." Juliana grins at me. I know I won't be able to shake her, so I nod.

ABBY: I have acquired a mentor against my will. The authorities feel I cannot handle middle school and require instruction.

MOM: A mentor is a good thing, sweetheart. How is your stomach?

ABBY: Digesting itself.

MOM: Don't cry wolf. How is it really?

ABBY: Not too bad.

9

After school, I get home and find Dad gone. When I send him a message, he replies that he's stuck at the DMV. I have two important missions to complete this afternoon, so I'm glad there are no parental units around to interfere.

I make a pile of peanut-butter-and-jelly sandwiches in the kitchen, wrap them in aluminum foil, and place them in my ridiculous plastic backpack along with three cans of Coke, my filled water bottle, and a big bag of Doritos. I also grab some soap, two towels, and a package with two new toothbrushes inside.

I walk to the marina, where I find Adam and Bix sitting on the deck of Dad's boat.

"How much longer?" Adam is asking Bix as I approach.

"Could be a day, could be a week," Bix is saying.

"A week?" Adam sounds unhappy—until he notices me. "Abby! You're back."

"And I brought dinner." I present them with the supplies.

"You're amazing!" Adam says between bites and gulps. "We were pretty hungry."

Bix doesn't say anything. He shoves almost an entire sandwich in his mouth at once and mumbles appreciative sounds. His oval tablet-thing is in his lap. It's a color I've never seen before—actually, it seems to *change* colors as I look at it. It shimmers. I wonder when I can ask Dad for a new phone. I want one like this, whatever it is. I bet *it* doesn't get weird messages from mysterious numbers.

"Are you guys American citizens?" I ask, perching in the middle of the boat's bow and drinking my own Coke.

"Not exactly," Adam answers. "Can we still be friends?"

"Sure," I say. "But where did you come from? You never told me. It might be important."

"We're citizens of the Alliance," Adam answers. "And of the Earth."

"There's no such thing as a citizen of the Earth,"

I say—and immediately realize how strange that sounds.

"Yes, there is," Bix says, having finally swallowed his sandwich completely and drunk half his Coke. "That was quite satisfying. I like the food here," he adds, eating from the bag of Doritos like I might snatch it away from him at any moment, which I might.

"What's the Alliance?" I ask. "Also, can I use your phone?" I want to get a closer look at it. "My battery is almost dead and I should probably text my dad to tell him when I'll be home."

"No!" he shouts. The bag of Doritos drops to the floor of the boat, forgotten. He repeats himself more quietly, holding his device close to his chest. "No. I'm sorry, you cannot. It's not a phone, it's a time-sorter, and it's very powerful."

"A time-*what*?"

A moment passes. I look back and forth between Adam and Bix, who seem to be communicating with their eyes. No one says anything.

"Abby, we should probably tell you something pretty important," Adam says. He reclines across the bow of the boat and seems relaxed. I notice Bix shooting him yet another frantic look. Adam catches Bix's eyes and shrugs.

"Okay," I say. "Sure. What's up?"

"We're from a different . . . time zone," Adam says. "The future, to be more accurate."

"The future?" I repeat blankly.

"Yes."

"As in, like, time travel?"

"Yes."

"You're telling me you're *time travelers*?" I narrow my eyes at the boys. "Very funny."

"It's true," Adam says. "But I don't blame you for not believing me."

"Good, because I don't."

"Bix voted not to tell you, but I voted we should. Hard to break a tie with only two people."

"And yet you seem to have broken it," says Bix darkly.

"I guess so." Adam smiles at me. He seems unperturbed. "Bix looked at all the models, and it turns out telling you the truth shouldn't mess anything up too badly in our timeline."

"But don't tell anyone else," Bix says, staring at his screen, which is flickering rapidly. "There is no model that looks good for us if you tell even one other person where we came from, at least right now."

"Don't worry, I won't," I say, imagining what Dad would do if I told him I was hiding two "time travelers" on his boat. I'd probably have to see the guidance counselor at school every single day or maybe just have all of my classes in his office until high school. "My mom says time travel is impossible."

Adam smiles. "Not impossible. Improbable."

My mind flickers with images from every futuristic movie and show I've ever seen. I wonder which one is their favorite. They're probably Comic-Con regulars, by the looks of them. "What year?" I ask, deciding to humor them.

"Mid-twenty-third century," Bix says. He picks up the chips again, looking resigned.

"That's . . . a long time from now. What's it like?"

"It's icy in some ways and completely kinked in others," Adam says.

I frown. "You have to at least *tell* me stuff if you want me to believe you. Like, what do I become when I grow up? What happens with the polar ice caps? Is the United States still around? Do I get my own flying car?"

"The less we tell you, the better," Bix says. "Besides, we were born more than two hundred years after you were. We have no idea what you become when you grow up."

"Could that time thingy tell me?" I lunge for it. Bix jerks away. The boat tips dangerously and he nearly drops the oval. He glares at me.

"Everyone, calm down!" Adam says. "Abby, I'm sorry, but Bix is right. It's better if we tell you as little as possible about the future. Even the tiniest detail will change how you act from this moment on and alter the flow of our history. And maybe even erase it completely."

"Sure, sure," I say. "I know how this works."

"You don't have to believe us," Adam says. "But I wanted to tell you because we're asking a lot of you. We're asking you to keep hiding us, without telling anyone about us, and we're not even sure how long we're going to be here. V isn't where—I mean when—we'd hoped to find her. She's unpredictable, it seems, no matter what century she's in. I'm hoping we can count on you to help us out until we can locate her."

I suddenly don't feel like joking around anymore. Adam seems totally serious. I consider the unusual clothes, the obliviousness to everyday realities like soda dispensers and cars, the mysterious device.

Maybe there's a tiny, tiny chance they're telling the truth. If not, they're the most convincing cosplayers of all time. Har.

I cross my arms and decide something: I'm getting my hands on the time-sorter and I don't care what Bix or Adam has to say about it.

Status report: much improved.

10

After leaving the marina, I don't feel like returning home. Adam and Bix's unbelievable story about where they came from has my mind reeling. They can't really be from the future, can they? But what's the point of claiming something so weird?

Who can I talk to about this? Olivia? No.

Dad? No.

The only person I know who could answer a question about quantum physics is Mom, but obviously I can't consult her. For one thing, she's hardly ever home.

But maybe there *is* someone else who has the answers I'm looking for.

I head over to Aunt Nora's again and ring the bell. My stomach is tight, but my curiosity about my aunt is stronger than my anxiety. She doesn't feel real, but then again nothing about this day feels real.

Nothing. I ring it again. Nothing. I decide to just keep ringing it until something happens.

After my fifth try, a speaker next to the bell crackles to life.

"Who is it?" A woman's voice. She sounds annoyed.

"Abby Monroe. Your, uh, niece?" I reply, clearing my throat. I have an impulse to run away. I'm not just scared now. I'm terrified.

"What do you want?" she replies. "I'm busy."

"Um. To meet you?"

"Why?"

"Because you're my . . . family?"

A long silence.

"Fine. Come in."

I hear the gate buzz and push it open, trembling as I walk onto the property.

I see immediately that the house and gardens are even more beautiful than my furtive spying earlier revealed. This place looks like it's been around for ages, like some kind of gothic dream plopped down in the middle of the desolate Florida swamp.

Nothing is neat or tidy. Instead, it's an explosion of life—flowers and giant leaves, live oak trees and hanging Spanish moss and winding shaded paths filled with stone benches and cherubic statues. There's an elaborate fountain in the middle of everything. I almost forget why I'm here; I'm so busy noticing all the details of my surroundings. My heart is beating very rapidly.

"So, you're Abby?"

I spin around to see a woman behind me wearing a large straw hat and gardening gloves. She's dressed simply, in loose-fitting khaki pants and a linen shirt with the sleeves rolled up. In her hand is a shovel. A Labrador with white fur around its nose and mouth sits by her side, regarding me placidly. The woman's face is difficult to read. She looks younger than I imagined.

"Ye . . . yes," I say, feeling like the unwelcome visitor I am. "Aunt Nora?"

"You can just call me Nora. This is Valentina," she says, nodding at the dog. "Let's have some tea and get this over with."

She turns around and walks toward the back of her house, where I see a shaded patio overlooking the canal. Nora gestures toward a cast-iron table and chairs that look extremely heavy and old. I take a seat and wait, not sure what to do with myself. It's unusual to be in the presence of an adult who doesn't want me around. I feel like I'm breaking a rule, even though neither of my parents said anything about *not* coming here.

Nora appears again, this time with a tray holding a pitcher of iced tea and two glasses. She pours the tea and sits down. I take a tiny sip. It's just a little sweet. Lemony. Good.

"So, here you are," Nora says, drinking her tea. I try not to stare at her, but it's difficult. She has hazel eyes that appear almost golden; it's unnerving. Her hair is a wild mixture of long blondish curls and silvery frizzy waves. She's strikingly beautiful, but feral-looking, like she might turn on me at any moment.

"Here I am. Against my will," I add, meeting her gaze and trying not to look away immediately.

She narrows her eyes. "Against your will? Did your mother send you down here? She's *unbelievable*."

"What? No. I mean, here in Florida. It's . . . not my thing." I realize I'm probably being rude. I wonder what she means about Mom.

"I see. You're right, Florida is terrible. It was beautiful once, but people ruined it." Nora takes a sip of her tea.

It feels good to be agreed with instead of told to find the positive. "People ruin everything," I say.

"You got that right." Nora won't make eye contact with me for more than a moment, which makes me uneasy and reminds me of Bix. The time traveler. *The time traveler.* My heart is pounding; I try to keep my breathing even and focus on what Nora has just said.

"I can see why you and Mom don't get along," I say, more to myself than to her.

"What do you mean?" she asks, still looking somewhere beyond my left shoulder instead of actually at me.

"Mom won't let me say anything negative, like, ever," I explain.

Nora doesn't reply to that. I drink my tea in silence for a few minutes until I can't resist asking my questions. "So, why is Mom angry with you?"

"You'll have to ask her," Nora replies.

"Is it true you never leave your house?"

She looks surprised. "No. Who said that?"

"Uh, no one. So, you're not agoraphobic?"

"No."

"Oh."

The conversation is stalling, and I can't bring myself to just blurt out, *In your professional opinion, is time travel a possibility?* I desperately want to see the inside of the mansion, so I ask to use the bathroom. Nora gestures to the door and says if I turn right, I'll find it. I'm sure she knows exactly what I'm up to, but she doesn't try to stop me from going in.

The house, on the inside, is nothing like the garden. It's orderly and modern-looking, with sleek, low furniture. I find the bathroom quickly and do my business. On the way back outside, I notice a room beyond the kitchen filled with computers and a blinking server rack. Every clock I see inside, on the stovetop, the microwave, and the wall, is set to an incorrect time: *11:53*.

Back outside, I finish my tea and thank Nora for letting me visit.

She doesn't invite me back.

11

T-minus 5 days to launch

Juliana is waiting for me outside the school doors the next morning. It's clear she takes being a mentor very seriously. I don't feel like talking that much; I slept very little last night and can't focus on anything besides the fact that I have two potential time travelers stowed aboard my dad's boat and I can't tell anyone.

"Is your locker okay?" Juliana asks, before even saying hello. "I forgot to ask you yesterday."

"Yes," I reply. "It's a locker."

"I picked up a school T-shirt for you," she says, pulling it out of her backpack. "Go Panthers!"

"Go Panthers," I repeat. "Thanks."

"I'll walk you to homeroom, then we'll meet up again at lunch. So, would you say you are more of an introvert or an extrovert? What do you do for fun?"

"Um." I blink at her.

"I'm an extrovert, which means being around people energizes me. I'm also an empath. I feel the pain of others more deeply than most people."

"Here's my homeroom." I duck into the first empty classroom I see, hoping Juliana will keep walking. She doesn't; she follows me right in. So much for feeling my pain.

"Wait a minute. I thought you were in Miss Bascom's homeroom. Mr. H gave me your schedule."

I sigh. "Oh. I thought this was her room."

"It's a good thing you have me, Abby," Juliana says, looking satisfied with herself. "Miss B's room isn't even *close* to here."

"Oops." I walk back out into the hallway. "I need to go to the bathroom before the bell rings. I'll see you at lunch!"

"Oh. Okay. Are you sure you can find your homeroom okay without me? I can wait."

"I'll find it. Thank you." I duck into the closest restroom and wave with what I hope is a friendly dismissal. Much to my relief, Juliana does not follow me right into a stall.

* * *

At lunch, I sit outside because that's allowed here. There are a bunch of picnic tables but no shade. I'm quietly beginning to die of sunstroke and plotting strategies for sneaking Bix's time-sorter away from him when Juliana asks if I've ever had a boyfriend.

"No," I admit. "Have you?"

"Of course," she says, as if every middle-school student is juggling seven potential love interests. "But I don't have one right now. I had to break up with Apollo two weeks ago because he wanted to go to second base and I'm not ready for any of that."

"Oh," I blink. "Um, I'm sorry?" I have no idea what to say. At my old school, no one in my class was hooking up at all. Everyone talked about it, but no one actually did anything. I think maybe we all knew each other too well. I miss them all so much. I wonder how Olivia is doing in band. I wonder if she still gets pesto stuck in her braces or if she decided to stop eating it.

"I'm not. You've got to respect yourself," Juliana says. "You know?"

"Yeah, I guess," I say, noncommittally. "So, why did you agree to be a mentor? Wouldn't you rather sit with your regular friends than with some rando?"

To my surprise, she blushes. "No, I like to help out," she says. "I was new when I was in fourth grade and I still remember how much it sucked."

"It does suck," I agree. I suddenly feel a surge of gratitude for Juliana. She maybe isn't destined to be my new best friend, but she is here.

"But you'll start to like it, I promise," she says, brightening. "I have. Have you been to KSC yet?"

"Yes, it's like my mom's church." Kennedy Space Center is the home of the huge Saturn V, the most powerful launch vehicle ever put into operation. Mom says seeing it gives her the same feeling as the cathedrals in Europe. We've been there at least five times in my life; I've touched the moon rock and paid my respects to the decommissioned Space Shuttle *Atlantis*.

"Are you serious?"

"Uh-huh." I smile a little bit at Juliana's horrified expression.

"*Church* is my mom's church," she says. "But she also really likes to spend time at the salon where my grandma works. You should come there with me sometime. The owner lets me do gel nails on myself if I sweep hair."

"Okay," I say, as I silently vow to never do that.

Even though I don't want to tell Juliana anything about Adam and Bix, I can't stop thinking about them. After taking a bite of my food and swallowing it, I ask, "Do you believe in time travel?"

"Sure," Juliana says. "One of my cousins says he thinks we'll know how to do it by the time I'm in college. But he also says he can communicate with his cockatiel telepathically, so . . ."

"Forget I asked," I say.

I notice a square sheet of paper tucked in the corner of my lunch sack. It's today's Florida attraction from my daily calendar: Weeki Wachee Springs State Park, featuring live mermaid shows.

Thanks, Dad.

12

When I get to the marina immediately after school, the boys aren't around. I panic. What if they've found V and left without saying goodbye?

My stomach seizes up and I try to do the breathing exercises one of the first counselors I ever had taught me. You're supposed to breathe in slowly to a count of four, hold the breath in for a count of seven, and breathe out.

The exercises don't work; they only make me slightly lightheaded. I yearn for the cool, crisp early fall air of Pennsylvania . . . not the swampy, inescapably moist heat all around me. I feel out of control and there's no one around to help. Pacing on the dock only makes me feel worse because everywhere I look, I see pieces of garbage floating in the water beneath me. Not even Mom could put a positive spin on someone deciding to throw their junk directly into the canals. *What is wrong with people? Don't they know that manatees will try to eat this stuff and die?*

I climb aboard Dad's boat, find his telescoping fish net, and begin scooping up all the trash and putting it in a bag to take home. After a half hour of this, my breathing returns to normal and my heart rate slows.

* * *

I spot Adam and Bix walking toward the boat. A cascade of relief floods over me. *They're still here.*

"Abby!" says Adam. "Good. We need to talk. We had to go find some calories and a charging station we could tap into for Bix's device."

"How did you pay for everything?" I ask, but I immediately reconsider. "Never mind. Don't answer that."

"We have a problem," Bix announces.

"Let's talk about it below deck, out of the sun," suggests Adam before Bix can get any further.

The cabin is musty-smelling and eight million degrees but otherwise okay. Bix continues: "The models I've been reviewing on my sorter today are showing a lower and lower probability of us finding V and returning to our timeline without disruption. I'm showing her pending arrival as T-minus nine days from now. Location imprecise."

"English, buddy," Adam says. Actually, Bix sounds like Mom, with his "T-minus" talk. I'm surprised this way of counting down is still used in the future.

"That *was* English," Bix replies. "We got here prematurely, and potentially nowhere near where V will be."

"What happens if you don't find her?" I ask.

Adam rubs his temples as he responds. "Not only will she be stuck here in the twenty-first century forever without the medical attention she needs . . . but my parents will kill me. And our entire history— your future—will be altered completely."

"As it is now, our starship doesn't exist on any causal chain," adds Bix. "It's merely one probability out of thousands."

"Which, come to think of it, will actually spare me my mom's wrath, so that's nice," says Adam.

"*Star*ship?" At this point, it's getting harder and harder to doubt the boys' story about where they've come from.

"Adam and I attend a Hadron Academy training mission camp," Bix says. "It's a program for young people who have particularly desirable aptitudes— aptitudes that must be honed so that we might, one day, crew a starship ourselves."

"Wow," I say.

"V accidentally focused herself—that is, transported herself—to the planet of Karq during a . . ." Bix pauses to cough. " . . . routine training exercise . . . where she then jumped through a time vortex. She's always been impulsive."

"That's Bix's way of giving a compliment," Adam says. "He has a huge crush on her."

"I do not. I merely admire V's spirit and intelligence," Bix protests.

"You've really got it bad, my friend," Adam teases.

"A time vortex," I repeat. I'm finding it difficult to keep up.

"Yup. Good ole V, noted troublemaker and object of Bix's affection, passed into *what was*," Adam says. "Everyone at camp is kinked."

"Kinked?" I ask.

"Bent out of shape. Flummoxed. But we managed to keep things quiet among the campers. We're hoping to resolve this without getting the authorities involved, or Vanessa will get in big, permanent-record-level trouble and may never get a starship commission of her own."

Bix says, "Adam and I decided to focus down to Karq and pass through the vortex as well, without notifying our instructors, Adam's parents, or senior crew."

"I know it seems risky not to involve any adults," adds Adam, "but if we had, V would've been kicked out of camp—forever."

"And that would be a misfortune for all who live in our time and beyond." Bix's face is grave. "She's got one of the best minds—sorry, Adam—I've ever encountered in my nine Earth years of life. She'll have a very illustrious career in the Hadron fleet one day if we can correct this static before it's too late."

"Intense," I manage. I blink at the boys, suddenly much more interested in the twenty-third century than I've ever been before. It never even occurred to me that there would actually *be* a future that far away. I want to see it.

"Yeah," says Adam. "And the truth is, Bix is downplaying the situation."

"I'm not downplaying anything. Our ship is blinkered," Bix says.

"What? What do you mean?" I ask.

"It's gone. Potentially. Probabilistically."

Adam takes it from there. "What we're doing is risky—coming here to retrieve my twin without any help. If we fail to locate her within a very narrow window of time, our entire ship will cease to exist, forever. The future is erased, and rewritten. It's fully creased."

"Creased?" I know that all I'm doing is repeating twenty-third-century slang, but I can't help it. Adam and Bix are speaking more quickly than I'm used to, and I don't want to miss anything.

"Messed up."

"You mean her arrival here messes up your present?"

Bix nods vigorously.

"We have to pinpoint V's arrival time and place and make arrangements to be there," Adam continues. "Until we do—until we get her back—our vessel, our beginning, *all that we know* is in jeopardy."

"Precisely." Bix nods. "Ordinarily, the sorter would allow us to calculate when and where V will exit the time vortex and materialize on Earth. But it isn't working properly. We need a computer. You do have computers in the early twenty-first century, yes?"

"Sure. But I'm still not following how the sorter thingy works . . ."

Bix sighs. "No clock for this. Look, Abby." For the first time, he turns the time-sorter screen toward me. "Just look, don't touch."

I see my opportunity and take it. I grab the time-sorter.

13

I'm instantly transported, standing on a platform overlooking a city—a soaring metropolis unlike anything in my wildest imaginings.

Bix's time-sorter is clutched in my hands, narrating the scene before me, but I don't hear any actual words being spoken out loud. Information appears as thoughts in my mind, descriptions unfurled in a soothing yet authoritative female voice that is definitely not my own. I understand—in a flash—that Bix has been using the sorter to quickly evaluate different, closely-related threads of time to try to figure out where V is located in my year, in my week, in Florida. He hasn't been doing it by reading words on his screen, he's been doing it by *feeling* his way across various ribbons of swirling atoms of cause and effect.

And what a feeling. I don't know where I am, exactly—it's not even clear if this city is on Earth—but I know it's where I want to live forever.

Welcome to Avia, says the voice in my head. *Population: 4.6 million. Year: 2272.*

There are enormous flying vehicles with bubble-like domed windows, moving placidly through the sky. Huge shining buildings, covered with massive vines, climb up to and beyond the clouds. They form towering spires in shapes that defy gravity. Everything looks alive, even the smooth raised highways looping in and around the shimmering structures. Sleek trains the same undulating opalescent color as the time-sorter glide along silently. There's no garbage anywhere, and hardly any right angles.

The air and the water are clean—better than clean. A subtle smell of citrus permeates the light breeze, and there's very little humidity. I look up, expecting to see some kind of bubble covering everything. But there's nothing there besides blue sky, puffy white clouds, and the occasional flying vehicle.

I see a staircase that leads down from my perch to street level, and I take it. I'm not sure how, but I'm instantly walking in a residential part of the city.

There are people everywhere, yet no cars on the roads. Everything is connected by cobblestone walking paths canopied by trees and flowering vines. Crystal-clear canals of pristine water are suspended above me. I don't understand how the water can float like that, but the effect is dazzling. I see kayakers, swimmers, and more than one small child float by on silver inner tubes. I have the sense of spending the entire morning swimming in an ocean. I feel at peace and yet more alive than I've ever felt.

I'm . . . optimistic.

The voice in my head says, *Humans learned long ago that the most truly fulfilled individuals are Creators, Explorers, and Caretakers. Consequently, these are the three main job categories in Avia. They take many forms. Creators design habitats, invent new games, write stories and plays, or grow gardens. Some paint, sculpt, compose and play music, decorate homes, or invent and test new kinds of recipes for others. They design the space stations now orbiting forty-two planets in our galaxy.*

Caretakers teach and care for the young, the old, and others in need of support. They keep order and fix broken code in machines with the help of AI. They are guides, docents, doctors, diplomats, professors, programmers, spiritual leaders, parents, therapists, coaches, and instructors.

Explorers are the scientists, the ship commanders, and the pioneers who work to map and understand the outer reaches of our galaxy.

There is very little crime, no poverty or hunger, and limitless free education. Most individuals live to the age of 115. Those who choose not to work do not have to; Avia is just one outpost of a post-scarcity world, powered by the energy of the stars. Food and shelter are freely available to all. Decentralized AI applications farm the fields, mine the asteroids, and perform cleaning and maintenance. All laws are voted on directly by every adult member of the city and expire on a rolling basis to prevent redundancies and gridlock.

The people moving around me look healthy and invigorated. Members of obviously alien species in a stunning array of shapes and sizes move among the humans. I think about how lonely we've all been on Earth, in my own time. How comforting it is to see for myself that in the future, human beings are no longer isolated in our galaxy.

The citizens of Avia have eliminated want and fear. They live in a world of creation, possibility, exploration, and abundance. Suspicion has been replaced by curiosity.

In my joy, I fail to note that the voice in my head, the narrator of the future, says nothing about solving the problem of war.

14

I blink, and I'm back in Dad's boat. More accurately, I'm sprawled out on the floor. Bix and Adam are standing over me, looking panicked.

Returning here—from there—is the hardest thing I've ever done. I feel thirsty, hungry, in pain. The overall sensation is like having a hundred-pound stone on my chest with no hope of ever being able to remove it.

"Was that . . . did I just see your time?" I whisper. "It's . . . beautiful."

"I told you not to touch the sorter!" Bix is shouting. His voice sounds far away, almost as if he's yelling at me underwater.

Only now do I understand Bix's desperation. All he wants to do is get back there. It's so much better than here. Clean, beautiful, *inspiring*. So, so much better. Something shifts inside of me, something big.

I want to live in that place, in that time.

**

Real progress toward a better future, Mom believes, comes from *iterative work*: Improve, test, repeat. Improve, test, repeat. She says she's not a genius at all—she's just willing to do whatever it takes, no matter how long it takes, to reach important goals and gain new knowledge . . . all while reminding me to "look on the bright side!"

Making the world a better place, as she sees it, comes from human beings doing things they'd only previously imagined. It comes from personal sacrifice and from not giving up *ever*. It comes from beginning to remember your own future. My fixation on dystopia, she says, is not helpful.

Now I understand she's deeply wrong. The fastest way to a good future is to skip ahead.

By, say, 250 years.

**

"I'll do everything I can think of to help you," I whisper to the boys, white-hot determination spreading through me like fire. "I'll bring you an entire refrigerator's worth of food. I'll take you to the library right after school tomorrow, so you can use the computers there. I'll do whatever it takes to help you find her. But you have to let me come back with you."

Bix starts to protest, but Adam cuts him off with a slicing gesture. "Deal."

We shake.

15

T-MINUS 4 DAYS TO LAUNCH

Traveling to the twenty-third century has made me think of my aunt in an entirely new way. I don't know her at all, but I kind of . . . love her.

She wanted what I want: to get off this crappy rock stuck in this backward time. When she was my age, NASA was pretty much the only game in town and she figured out a way to play.

Now, she's sitting on the sidelines. I feel bad for her, but my plan isn't to change the way she spends her time.

I don't have a plan. I just wish I could tell her— tell anyone—where I've been and where I'm going.

Late that night when I should be asleep, I dig out another message she sent my mom twenty years ago.

Dear Anna,

Back when I was in college, it was very
intimidating to walk into a room of other
engineers. I'd often sit in the back. If I heard
someone say something factually incorrect,
I wouldn't correct them in front of everybody.
I would talk to them separately later. I didn't
realize that it was my job to correct the facts
in real time. Later, when I'd present my work
in design reviews, my colleagues and management
and mentors and product assurance people would
all try to find the weaknesses. They weren't
attacking me or my ideas; they were simply
trying to ensure that the design was the best
it could possibly be and that we, as a team,
were learning from previous mistakes.

It took an incredible amount of courage
to keep trying, yet I felt it would be too
embarrassing to admit to anyone in my life,
mostly my parents, that I wanted to switch
careers.

I was too stubborn to fail. And I liked
learning about how stuff works. If you have
a natural curiosity about how and why things
work, engineering is fun. I know you're deciding

what to do right now and I want to make a pitch for my field. You can make things and have a real influence. I should admit to you, however, that sometimes I really hate my job. I'm not working on any interesting technical challenges at the moment. Often my day is made up of teleconferences, teleconferences, and more teleconferences. I think about quitting NASA sometimes.

But what else would I do? I look at things I like, that I'm good at, and that I want to learn more about but I keep returning to this: only shuttle launches give me chills. I like the math. I like the technical problems and finding a solution that meets a need. I like having discussions that are mini-negotiations about the trade-offs of this design versus this design. I also like the fact that I've worked here for fourteen years. People ask me questions. They value my opinion on how to do things better. I'm used to having a certain amount of clout.

Don't let any of what I've said here alter your trajectory, Anna. These are all just circumstances. You are the rocket.

~N

You are the rocket. I like that. My mom *is* a rocket. A very, very annoying rocket, but also an impressive one.

I'm feeling a lot different than I usually do. It's as if the cells in my body are in an altered order, as if the waves in my brain are vibrating at a new frequency. Even the heat outside doesn't bother me. I feel it for what it is: pure possibility. The sun is bathing us all in the energy human beings will use to do what they want, to go where they want, to create what they need. It's all around us, free, infinite. Just there for the taking like gold lying in a stream.

I need to make sure Adam and Bix find V in time so that they can take me to the twenty-third century. Maybe once I get settled there, I can come back for Mom and Dad. But for now, I have to stay focused: for starters, I'm taking Adam and Bix on a field trip to the library after school tomorrow. And if the computers there don't do whatever Bix needs them to do . . . I need a backup plan.

Maybe Nora will have some ideas. But how will I get her to talk to me? She wasn't exactly welcoming the last time I stopped by.

I decide to do what Dad does with me when he's trying to get me to help him with yard work: bribery.

"Juliana, I need help with something," I say the next day at lunch, instead of answering her question about what kind of conditioner I use in my hair. (Answer: whatever conditioner my dad buys at the grocery store, I don't know.)

She looks at me, startled. I don't usually initiate a new topic of conversation between us. Not because I'm that much of a jerk, but because she's never quiet for the three-second interval it would take for me to think of a question to ask or something new to say. I mainly just answer her questions or chew my food while she relates all the latest gossip from her mom's pet boarding business or her grandma's salon. About people I've never met. And their dogs.

I now realize that Juliana mentors new kids because they're an easy target, a captive audience. But I don't mind. I've decided I like Juliana. Especially since I learned I'm only going to be putting up with her for another few days before beating it to Avia. Visiting the future has made me a much kinder person. I feel like I've won the lottery and I just haven't cashed in my ticket yet.

"Anything," she says, licking her fingers. She is polishing off a brownie.

"I have this aunt I don't really know who lives

not too far from here, and I want to do something nice for her. Like, bring her some food, or something like that, so she'll feel like inviting me in to her house. Any ideas?"

"Ooh, sure." Juliana nods. "There's this stand at the farmer's market, it's run by friends of my mom's, and they sell guava-and-cheese pastelitos. I've never seen a person not buy a second one after having the first. We can get a whole box of them on Saturday if you want. Hey! That reminds me. Do you want to come to our pet hotel that morning and meet my family? The market is right nearby. We can play with the dogs for a while and check on my favorite, Ruby. She's about to have a litter of puppies!"

My mentor grins at me, her face full of dimples and cheer. I'm in such an unusual mood that I nod and smile right back. It even goes all the way to my eyes for a change. "It's a plan. Thanks, Juliana. I knew you'd know what to do."

* * *

Later that afternoon, as fast as I can run from school, I return to the boat. "Who's ready to see some twenty-first-century computers?"

Bix is rubbing his eyes. It appears the boys have been sleeping. I don't feel guilty at all about waking them. We've got no time to waste.

"Finally," says Bix. "We've been waiting all day for you to return, because we are out of power and not sure where we can go where we will be inconspicuous."

"We went back to the Checkers when you were at school," Adam says. I see a smile in his eyes. "But the hand dryer in the bathroom kinked Bix out."

"It did not kink me out," Bix protests. "I just did not enjoy it."

"Also, we couldn't find any outlets," Adam adds. "No luck at McDonald's either."

"Actually, we did find one there—a very primitive one—but we were asked to exit for not buying anything. Why is everyone here so fixated on money?" Bix says. "It's a completely imaginary concept. If the store manager was interested in extracting something of value from me, we could've simply had a conversation. I have much of value to teach."

I glance at Adam, who rolls his eyes, but in a nice way.

"Money is . . . kind of a big deal right now," I try to explain. "If you don't have it, or a way to get it, or parents who earn it, you're in a never-ending struggle. Lots of people are hungry, without a safe place to live or a way to get help when they're sick."

Both boys stare at me. "That's barbaric," Bix says. "Feudal."

"Why can't it be fixed?" Adam asks.

"I'm not sure," I admit. Mom thinks SpaceNow is good for humanity, but could all those billions of dollars spent on rockets be used for something else? Who is going to benefit from the technology and who is going to be left behind?

Dystopia.

"If I had any money, I'd give it to you," Bix says solemnly. "I didn't realize your society was organized in this manner. My knowledge of Earth's economic history is quite limited, I realize."

"That's okay."

I don't know how to tell Bix I don't need any money without sounding awkward. I'm the girl who went to private school for most of my life, and if I threw a big enough fit, I probably could again. SpaceNow is paying my mom. A lot.

And I benefit. A lot.

It's kind of nauseating to consider all the ways the twenty-first century is unfair *in my favor*. I feel like I often do: that I should be doing something, doing more, taking some action to make things better, but I don't know where to start or how to get to the root of it all.

So instead, I think about Avia and that soothing voice I heard in my head when I visited. I have a goal . . . to leave these kinds of problems where they belong. In the distant, remote past.

And to reach that goal, I just have to focus on the next logical step. "We can charge your device at the library, and you can check out the computers there. Sound good?"

"Affirmative," Bix says.

I text Dad using the last two percent of battery life on my phone to tell him I'm going to the library in our neighborhood with some new friends. A moment later I get a single-word text, again from a long string of numbers: *FORMATION*.

What does it mean?

"Do either of you send text messages?" I ask, showing both Adam and Bix my phone screen.

"What's a 'text,' exactly?" Adam asks.

"Oh. It's a written digital message. We send them to each other on our phones. But usually you get them from people you *know*, not weird numbers that are like twenty-five digits long."

Adam nods, puzzled. "I haven't figured out how to get my communication beacon to work with your cellular network."

"I have," Bix says. "I'm just not interested in sending messages to you. Sorry."

I sigh. "I need to take this thing in and get it fixed or something."

We pile off the boat, and I lead the other two away from the marina. "Explain to me how the time vortex works," I say. My journey to the twenty-third century has made me voracious for knowledge. I want to know everything Adam and Bix know, immediately, so I can stop thinking about the present.

"The vortex," Adam explains, pinching the bridge of his nose like I've seen Mom do a hundred times, "is an incredibly rare spot in the galaxy. It's not like time travel is a regular thing for us."

"Improbable, but not impossible?"

"Precisely." Adam smiles. "For several hours before V focused herself out of camp, it was the source of a lot of time displacement aboard our ship—in fact, I'm now sure it's the reason V was acting so strangely. I mean, more strangely than usual. Our instructors were trying to investigate it without compromising our syllabus or our vector that morning. But all I can actually say about it is it's impossible to explain by any science you—or even I—could understand."

"Try me," I say.

"Well, from what we can tell, the vortex on Karq is specifically linked to Earth; when we entered it on Karq in our time, we rematerialized on Earth in the past. If we enter it on Karq in *this* time, we'll end up on Earth in our time."

"But wait—how are you supposed to get to Karq now? It's not like you can just rent a space shuttle."

"By focusing," says Adam. "I think you might call it teleporting. It takes a lot of effort, but we can transport ourselves—and/or anything we're touching or holding—to another location, pretty much anywhere in the galaxy."

"Are you serious?"

"I've only done it once before in my entire life. It's really draining, even when our communication beacons are working at full capacity."

He taps a small spot behind his ear. I see that the skin there is slightly raised in the shape of a triangle.

"That's a communication device?" I ask. I can't imagine trading my iPhone in for a weird implant. So what if the phone's a little glitchy from time to time?

"Yep. Kind of like a neural lace, which you'll

hear all about in a few years or decades, I think. It allows us to communicate telepathically, without having to say anything aloud—if we want to. It's like being on Karq, only all the time." I don't know what that part means, but he's still talking. "We can also look up information, get an AI assist, whatever we need. It's pretty great."

"Whoa," I say, newly staggered. "So, not only can you transport yourselves across the galaxy, but you two can talk about me without saying anything out loud?" I look back and forth at the two boys nervously.

"Yes," Bix sighs, sounding bored. "But don't worry, we haven't said anything you've not heard. He thinks you're pretty and smart, I think you're moderately helpful but thirty percent likely to derail our entire mission. And five percent likely to get us all killed."

"Um, thank you?" I say to Bix. I blink, processing that. *Killed?* To Adam, I say, "Thanks," but much more softly.

"It's not that important what *we* think of *you*, Abby," Adam says. "A much more interesting question is what you think of us. We're completely lost without you."

"I think you're both fascinating," I say. Understatement. "Isn't having a device embedded in your brain kind of, I don't know, invasive?"

"Not really," Adam says. "We can turn it off at will. It's less bothersome than holding something up to your face, I think." We arrive at the library and Adam looks around. There are maybe twenty people scattered outside the doors and in the lobby of the building. About half of them are staring down at their phones. Scratch that. More than half.

"Right. That's a good point. Um, Bix, I think we can charge our—"

"Computers!" he says. He heads right for a line of monitors along one wall. Adam and I follow, but at a slower pace. Bix sits down at a terminal and begins typing. Unfortunately, he is immediately tapped on the shoulder by a librarian, who points to the sign that says users must sign up for a computer time slot at the front desk before getting started.

I have a local library card and use it to get Bix squared away. Adam and I sit at a table nearby, and I plug in my phone with a charger from my backpack.

"So, are all these people here to read books and learn things?" Adam asks incredulously. "I never studied the early twenty-first century in school."

"Probably not all of them," I say, looking at a kid who is clearly playing a video game on the computer next to Bix. "But some of them, sure."

"I like it here." Adam grins at me. "I know there are a lot of problems, but right now, in this moment, I like it."

"I'm glad," I say sincerely. "But I don't. I really don't. That stuff I told you about money was just the tip of the iceberg."

He looks alarmed. "Are your people at war?"

"War? Well, sort of always, but that's not . . ." Obviously I'm doing a poor job of explaining the pain, the unfairness, the inequality and suffering of our current time. I suddenly feel silly.

"I'm sorry, Abby," Adam says, and touches my hand with his own, partially covering my fingers with his. "Sometimes I forget that when we visit new places in the galaxy, we usually arrive right in the middle of something important. Every person's life is so incredibly complex. I'm sure there's a lot going on for you right now."

I'm surprised by how much I appreciate his understanding, which is so different than Mom's blunt-force approach to handling my emotions. I choke up a little but manage to steady my breathing.

I want to explain to Adam what's been going on, but I'm not sure where to start. I'm not used to my feelings swinging around so wildly. In just one day, I've gone from anxious to elated and back to anxious again, and I don't even really know why. "Well, like I said before, we just moved here," I say. "I miss my friends, I miss my grandparents, I miss the cool fall air. I've been very homesick," I admit, trying to sum up the last few weeks in just one word. "But that's not even really the whole problem. It's more . . . I feel like no one really believes the future is going to be better than the past and I think everyone's in pain because of it. Including me, until you two showed up."

Adam nods. "I suppose the last thing you need is to deal with two boys who are lost in space."

"I'm happy to deal with two boys who are lost in space," I say. "You guys are my ticket out of here."

"Right, but . . ." Adam trails off. I choose to ignore it, thinking instead of the crystal-clear Avia sky. "But about homesickness. Been there. It's kinked. Let me tell you what my dad told me about it—something that helps."

"Okay," I say. "I'm listening."

"You know how when you've lived somewhere a long time, or your entire life even, you collect about four thousand data points about that place? Like, little things. Things you don't even think about, but just know? The stair that creaks. The sign in the window with some little kid's sticker on it that's been there forever?"

"Yes. Yes. That's the problem." I nod. "I miss all that stuff. Even the small stuff! Even the little kid's sticker." I sniffle and feel deeply embarrassed when my eyes fill with tears. I'm flooded with memories of home. Of the color of Olivia's new glasses, of the smell of the honeysuckle bushes lining my old driveway. I grab my still-charging phone and send Olivia a sparkle emoji just to let her know I'm thinking of her. She sends me back a DNA helix and a yawn; she must be doing homework.

"Hey, hey, I get it. I know," Adam says. "But, listen. You can make a new list. I've done it a dozen times, each time I have to live on a new planet or spend time on a different starship. I start right away."

"You do?" I ask, quickly wiping my eyes with the sleeve of my T-shirt. "How?"

"I just start adding stuff I notice about my new surroundings. The silliest stuff I can find. Like, for one, the door sticks between airlocks seven and eight on the *Audacity*. You know? The longer the list of data points gets, the better you feel."

"I like that idea," I say, smiling a little. "Here, there's a Publix grocery store every half mile. They're seriously everywhere." I think longingly of the co-op I used to visit all the time back home. It smelled like soap and organic produce. "Anyway, they all have a big scale in the front of the store, right when you walk in. And they're all calibrated just a little bit wrong. I've checked."

Adam laughs. "Maybe they're set to Moon gravity."

"Maybe," I say sheepishly. Who checks grocery store scales? I'm such a dork.

"That's exactly what I'm talking about," he says with a grin. "You get it. Add at least one thing every day, and you'll feel a tiny bit better until you feel completely smooth. I promise."

"It doesn't matter anyway." I remember now. "I'm getting out of here. Is there even a *Florida* in the twenty-third century?"

Adam opens his mouth, but I cut him off. "You know what, you don't have to answer that question. I don't even care!"

I suppress a flicker of doubt in my mind, just as I've seen Mom do a dozen times when she has to muscle through a tough decision. I'll never see Olivia again. Or Jones.

Or—unless I figure out a way to drag them along too—Mom and Dad.

I blink and hold my breath for a second longer than usual before I let it out.

Adam's expression is unreadable as he tells me he's going to check on Bix.

16

"These computers are feeble, even by twenty-first-century standards." Bix says, after he's given up on whatever he was trying to do. It turns out the Brevard County library budget does not provide computing power equal to the requirements of a twenty-third-century space-faring genius child.

"Bix! Don't be rude," Adam admonishes.

"Sorry. Before the machine I was using overheated, I did make a little progress," Bix says, putting his oval screen back in the small pouch at his side. "I believe we have about eight days before V arrives."

"Excellent," Adam says, clapping his hands. "Then in the meantime, we can relax. We can go to the beach!"

I smile.

"But we still don't know *where* she'll arrive," Bix says, his brow furrowed with worry. "New York, India, Greenland? At the speed we were seeing on Karq, time and place were shifting inside that vortex too rapidly for me to . . ."

"I know, I know," Adam says, waving away his friend's worries. He's an optimist like my mother, I see. Only his optimism doesn't annoy me as much for some reason. "But I trust your calculations, B. You think she'll come here, she'll come here."

Bix seems to relax slightly. "It *is* most likely that she'll arrive in this general vicinity." He adds, as if to himself, "And if not, we have no hope." He looks at his feet. "It's frustrating. If I could hook into our ship's computer for just a few moments . . . but I can't. The ship is only a probability right now."

"It's okay, Bix. I'm expecting too much. Let's go back to the marina for the night and relax."

Bix begins to protest, but I interrupt. "I get it," I say. "You need more power. And I know where you can get it. My mom's work."

My phone buzzes.

DAD: Are you still at the library? Do you need me to come get you?

ABBY: Yes, I'm still at the library. I'll be home in 15 minutes. Is Mom there?

DAD: Not yet.

ABBY: Okay, I'll text her. What's for dinner?

DAD: Takeout pad thai

"I have to go home for dinner," I tell the boys. "But I bet I can get my mom to drive us to work with her tomorrow. She goes in even on Saturdays, because she works for this intense aerospace company called SpaceNow."

Bix sits up straight, and Adam blurts out, "Your mom works for SpaceNow?"

"You've . . . heard of it?"

"Of course! It was covered in our first-level Earth history class."

Bix is nodding vigorously. "The technology there should be adequate. If we can gain access to it."

"I bet my mom would love to give us a tour," I say. "And then she'll probably get distracted by the actual work she has to do, which would mean you could get some unsupervised time with her computers."

"Abby," says Adam, looking impressed, "this sounds like a plan."

I give the boys directions to my house and tell

them to meet me there tomorrow around noon. Mom usually heads to the office right after lunch on Saturday.

But before that, I'll have to meet up with Juliana and weasel my way back into Nora's mansion. It's a good thing it's the weekend.

I have way too much to do to deal with seventh grade right now.

* * *

ABBY: Would you be able to give my two friends and me a tour of SpaceNow tomorrow afternoon? They're also really into space.

MOM: SURE! I'd be happy to!

ABBY: Thanks, I know you're really busy.

MOM: Never too busy to share our vision with some eager young minds!

I start to roll my eyes, but I feel a little wave of guilt. On a scale of one to ten, how bad is it to pretend to be interested in your mom's work to escape life in the twenty-first century?

I'm thinking, like, a five.

17

"Dad, can you give me a ride?" I ask the next morning. It's only eight-thirty, but he's already outside, filling in cracks in the stucco of our house with some kind of goopy substance. He has his phone propped up on a ladder next to him, playing music.

"You're up early," he says, pausing his song. "A ride where?"

"To my friend Juliana's family's pet boarding place. It's called the Fur Seasons." I mumble this last part, but he hears me anyway.

"The *Fur* Seasons?"

"Yeah."

"Nice."

"Yeah." I pull on flip-flops and put my hair into a bun. "So, can I have a ride? I said I'd help exercise the dogs this morning."

"Sure. I'm glad you're making friends. Let me just wash my hands."

Ten minutes later, Dad stops his CRV in front of a long, low building made of white cinder blocks. It doesn't look that fancy, but there are baskets of flowering plants hanging all across the front at regular intervals. I double check the address, and a moment later I see Juliana waiting for me on a bench wearing a T-shirt with a logo I don't recognize. She waves enthusiastically.

"Thanks, Dad. I'll see you later," I say and give him a quick salute as I hop out of the car. He waves to me as he turns the car around and heads back home.

"Hey," I say to Juliana.

"Hey!" she replies. "So, this is it. What do you think?"

"I like the flowers."

"Me too." She smiles. "Let's go inside."

An older version of Juliana is at the front desk drinking coffee and petting a little light-tan-and-white dog in her lap. "Abby, this is my mom. Mom, Abby."

"Nice to meet you, Mrs. . . ." I trail off, shaking

the friendly-looking woman's hand. The small dog jumps down and trots over to me, sniffing my ankles. She is so adorable—fluffy and happy-looking like a little living teddy bear. I see she has a swollen belly. The dog lies down on the cool floor tile and places her head right on my feet.

"Rivera. Nice to meet you too, Abby. Looks like you've gotten the Ruby seal of approval."

I reach down to pet Ruby's head. "Cute. What kind of dog is she?"

"A Maltipoo," Juliana answers. "Maltese and poodle."

"How come she's not with the other dogs?" I ask.

"She lives here full time. She runs the place."

"Oh, she's yours." I nod. "I see."

"Yes," Juliana says. "But it didn't start that way. She got left here by her owners. That happens some- times. We usually call the humane society."

"Oh." I frown.

"But Juliana begged me to keep this one, and I'm glad we did because it turned out she was carrying puppies," Mrs. Rivera says. "Even though she's not much of a watchdog."

"That's really sad," I say, petting Ruby's head again. "Someone just left her? Who does that?"

"I know, right?" Juliana says. "But she's home now."

"Are her nails painted red?" I ask, surprised.

"Yeah." Juliana sounds kind of sheepish. "She likes it. I helped my little sister do it."

"None of the other dogs here participate in Isabel's pet salon," Mrs. Rivera assures me with a smile.

We all stare at Ruby and her belly for a moment and I feel the old familiar knot in my stomach. *How can someone just leave their pet behind? How can people be so terrible?* I bet no one ever abandons their dogs in Avia.

Ruby licks my big toe, and I snap out of it. She's okay. She's being taken care of by nice people, regardless of what century it is. "Wanna meet some more dogs?" Juliana asks. "Let's each pick one to walk around the block. We can let out the rest to play in the yard."

"Sure."

Juliana gives me a tour of the whole pet resort, and it's very nice. There's one big room partitioned into little enclosures for each dog—she explains they only take smaller breeds under forty pounds. Each enclosure has a dog bed, toys, a thick blanket, and a small door that goes directly outside into the play yard in the back.

I choose a medium-sized spaniel named Sasha who is enjoying her last day at the Fur Seasons, and Juliana picks a Shiba Inu called Peeta who she says was just checked in yesterday. Juliana tells me the Fur Seasons is very popular with cruise ship travelers since most cruise ships don't allow dogs.

We clip leashes onto Sasha's and Peeta's collars and set out for a walk around what turns out to be a very loooong block. The two dogs walk nicely together, sniffing at the air and at the ground but moving at the same pace. They've been well trained.

"So, this is what you do on the weekends?" I ask.

"Yup. Actually, every day before school too."

"Cool. Does your mom pay you?"

"No. But I wouldn't want her to. It's a family business," Juliana says. "We all have to work together if we want it to stay open. My brothers help out too. And my abuela—my grandma—when she's not doing nails or highlights at the salon."

I'm surprised. If *my* mom owned a pet hotel and I worked at it every day, I'd probably demand she pay me. But I remember my conversation with Adam and Bix—about how lots of people don't have as much money or security as my family—so I don't say this out loud.

Instead I ask, "What do you do if a dog is scared? If they don't want to walk or play with the other dogs?"

"I just give them a treat and see if they'll let me pet their fur," Juliana says. "Usually, I can get them to relax. I'm good at it."

"So, is that kind of, like, your thing?" I ask. I feel embarrassed. Like I'm Juliana's little lost puppy.

"I guess so," she admits. "Some people are good at sports. I'm good at being nice and taking care of animals."

"Oh," I say. We walk a few yards in silence. "I'm not sure what I'm good at."

"It's okay," Juliana assures me. "Maybe it's not just one thing."

I nod but don't reply. I think about the three categories of people in the future: explorers, caregivers, and creators. I have no idea which one I might be.

What if I get to Avia and feel just as lost as I do here? What then?

18

Juliana and I exercise three more pairs of dogs before it's time to go to the farmer's market to buy a box of guava-and-cheese pastelitos for Nora. I pay for them using my phone (which is thankfully behaving today), give Juliana two, and text Dad to pick us up. He drops Juliana back off at the Fur Seasons and I ask him to take me to Nora's.

"Really?" he asks. "I thought Mom told you she didn't like to be bothered."

"We're friends," I say, even though it's not really true. "She asked me to get these for her." I lift up the box slightly.

"Oh. I didn't realize that." He looks at me, confused, but seems to make a decision not to question me. "Okay. Well, don't hang out there for long if she's in the middle of something."

I promise him I won't. "I'll be home in a little bit," I say when we pull up to her address. "It's not too far to walk. Tell Mom not to leave for work without me, though. She said she'd give a tour to two of my friends today."

"Aren't you becoming popular? I'm so proud of you!"

"Gross," I say. But I smile a little. Sometimes this thing happens to me where I feel like a grown-up stuck in a twelve-year-old's body. This is one of those times. Of course, now that I know time travel is real, it doesn't seem that weird at all.

"See you soon." He waves as I hop out and shut the door.

My stomach clenches for a moment. What if I can't come back from the future and bring him with me? What if, once I reach Avia, I never see him again?

***

The outer walls of Nora's house look as unwelcoming as ever. I listen for a moment, hoping to hear Valentina rustling on the other side of the wall, or maybe even Nora gardening. Instead, all I hear is complete silence. I ring the buzzer. Nothing. Again. Nothing. Again.

"Yes?"

Progress! I only had to press the button three times. "It's Abby."

"Abby?" I'm not sure, but I think I hear Nora sigh. "What do you need?"

"Nothing. I brought you guava-and-cheese pastelitos. They're still warm."

"Did your mother put you up to this?" Nora asks. My brain tickles; she asked me the same thing the last time I visited.

"No. She doesn't even know I'm here. Why?"

"Anna doesn't respect my boundaries or listen when I say I'm done arguing. And now—surprise, surprise—she lives just down the street from me."

"I know," I say. "She can be the *worst* sometimes."

I think I hear a small snort through the intercom, but the gate buzzes and I push it forward, like last time. The grounds of Nora's property are quiet. Just like before, the air feels as if it's made of different molecules in here than it is outside the walls. It's still oppressively humid, but there's a stillness to it that feels right. The density and variety of flowers and trees make the space cooler than the air on the other side. I see a dragonfly flit past my nose and a cluster of plump bumblebees drinking from a flowering bush. I'm the only thing in the environment that doesn't belong, but I don't want to leave.

I feel as if I could sit down in the middle of it all and think of nothing and be okay.

I lift up the heavy pewter knocker on the front door as gingerly as I can. A middle-aged woman I don't recognize opens the door. She's wearing an artist's smock and glasses pushed up on her head. Her skin is brown and her eyes are friendly. "Hello?"

"Hi. I'm Nora's niece, Abby. I brought pastries."

"How lovely! I'm Carla, her painting instructor. We were just finishing up." Carla gestures for me to follow her. Two easels are set up on the patio off the kitchen where Nora and I had tea together last week. I see Nora behind one of them with glasses on her nose and a paintbrush in her hand. Valentina is at her feet. Nora nods at me, her expression neutral. "Abby."

"Nora," I return. "Thanks for letting me in." I'm not sure where to set the box I'm holding. The patio table is covered in paints. I peer at the two canvases. The one before Nora is supposed to be of a bird-of-paradise, I think, but it's . . . not good. The proportions are wrong somehow, but not in any way that looks deliberate. Nora sees where my eyes have landed and makes a dissatisfied noise.

"I know. It's terrible. What can I do for you?"

I'm not sure what to say. I want to ask Nora if she believes time travel is possible, but meeting Carla has thrown me off balance. "I just came to visit," I say.

"Did I mention when we met that I don't generally like children?" Nora sets down her paintbrush and removes her glasses. "You're nosy and persistent."

At this, Carla laughs. She sits down at her own canvas and I see that her painting is of a glass of water. It looks beautiful. Somehow, she's managed to use every color of the rainbow and yet make the water she has painted look wet.

"I'm sorry," I say, placing the box of food onto one of the patio chairs. Valentina raises her head and sniffs, but stays where she is at Nora's feet. "I *am* persistent. Mom wants to ignore you, so all I want to do is the opposite."

"I see." Nora seems to soften. A hint of a smile appears in her eyes.

I'm not sure what to say next, so I settle on flattery. "I'm trying to help some friends solve a difficult problem. I was thinking maybe you could help. Is it true you're a genius?"

Carla pauses her painting and looks at Nora, who shakes her head. "It's not true. Sorry."

"Oh. Well, that's okay. Can I just watch you paint for a while?" I like being here. So much so that I almost forget about Adam and Bix and Avia.

"I suppose. Why don't you make yourself useful first and go make some coffee to go with those pastries? The machine is on the counter next to the fridge and the coffee itself is in a canister right next to it."

"Okay." I like how my aunt just assumes I know how to work a coffeemaker. I don't, but I like having the chance to poke around in her cool kitchen alone. The clock on the stove is still stopped at 11:53, just like before. So is the one on the microwave. How do you even make it *do* that?

I figure out the percolator after staring at it for a minute (and by googling *How does a percolator work?* with my phone, which helps a lot). After a few minutes of listening to the old machine gurgle, I see that the pot is full. I find two mugs in the cupboard after opening nearly every cabinet door, fill them, and return to the patio. Carla is packing up her paints.

"I'd love to stay and chat with you, Abby," she says, "but I have another lesson at eleven. It was so nice to meet you. You'll have to drink my coffee."

Carla smiles and is gone. She leaves her painting of the glass of water behind. I walk over to it.

"She's good," I say.

"Yes," Nora agrees. "Very."

"So, you paint?"

"I'm not sure I'd call it that. I *try* to paint."

"You just do pretty much whatever you want all the time," I remark. Nora doesn't seem old to me, at least not old enough to be retired, although I guess technically she *is* in her sixties. I'd retire right now if Mom would let me.

"Yes. I recommend it. I'm constantly surprised how few people try it."

"Mom says people have to find their purpose," I say.

Nora rolls her eyes and swats away a pair of love-bugs hovering near her face. Juliana told me they'll be everywhere along the coast in September.

"You don't think that's true?"

"I think you should listen to your mother," she says. "But once you get to be my age, you can decide for yourself."

"I'd rather decide for myself now."

"Smart girl." Nora turns away from me and dabs her paintbrush on a wet paper towel. She begins cleaning up, and I feel like I'm being dismissed, right as things are getting interesting.

I want to tell her what I've seen in Bix's oval, tell her I know more about what's going to happen than maybe any other person she's ever met in the history of her entire life. But she probably wouldn't believe me.

"What if I decide to leave behind everything and everyone I've ever known and do something completely different?" I ask instead. "If I know it's going to be way better than anything I could do if I stayed where I am?"

Nora shrugs. "I'm not sure why you're asking *me*."

I'm not totally sure either. I just want to know what she thinks. I want to know everything about Nora, mainly because she doesn't want to tell me anything. "Because you've *done* that. First you moved from Pennsylvania to Florida to work for NASA, and then you left NASA and . . ." I make a sweeping gesture. "You do your own thing here now."

"Well, I don't have any wisdom to share with you, Abby. Sorry. But you seem like a very confident child so I'm sure you don't need my advice."

I frown. I wish she'd stop calling me a child. "I'm not confident. I have anxiety," I blurt out.

"Who doesn't?" Nora replies.

"You too?"

"Here's the thing about anxiety, Abby. The thing I wish someone had told me a long time ago: anxiety is like opposable thumbs. It's part of the package, part of being human. It's something that most of us just *have*. Especially when there are good reasons to worry. You're probably just paying attention more than a lot of people."

"That's the most you've ever said to me at one time," I say.

"So it is."

"But it doesn't feel like I'm in charge of my anxiety like I'm in charge of, you know, my thumbs. It's more like *it* is in charge of *me*."

"I'm sorry to hear that." Nora returns her attention to tidying up. "Still, if I were you, I wouldn't wish to take away my unease completely. It's a reaction to the world that often makes sense. And that restlessness, that refusal to be complacent, is what makes us who we are."

"I've never thought of it that way before," I say. I don't usually like the way that I am or the way that I feel. Nora telling me to find a way to accept it is . . . annoying, but less so than Mom telling me to *apply myself*.

"You don't have to listen to a word I say, of course. I'm just an old lady who never leaves her house."

"I think you're very interesting."

Nora turns away from her canvas and looks at me. "You're not so bad yourself."

"So, when my stomach is in knots or I can't sleep, what should I do?"

"What you're asking is something every human has asked themselves and others more than perhaps any other question: *Where can I find comfort? How?*"

"Yeah," I say, thinking of how recently I googled a question very much like this one: *Will we be okay?* "How?"

"I told you, I don't have any answers," Nora says. "Every person has to answer that question for themselves, and they do so in a billion different ways. You could paint. Write. Try to stay in the present moment. Breathe."

I stop myself from rolling my eyes. Staying in the present moment is the opposite of what I plan to do. "I see," I finally say, disappointed. This advice isn't really new or helpful.

"But I will tell you one thing," Nora says. "Anna—I mean, your mother—is just as anxious as you are. If not more." Nora is done cleaning up and heads for the patio door. "You should talk about your feelings with her; you two are so much alike."

I blink, surprised. "Um, what? No, she's not anxious. She's all about seeing the positive. She drinks green smoothies every single day and runs marathons for *fun*."

Nora's eyes crinkle at the corners. "I guess that's one way to solve the problems of the world. Look, Abby, life is half and half, good and bad. I hope someday Anna goes a little easier on herself and slows down. Or at least learns to paint with all the colors."

"What about you? Don't you ever worry?"

A shadow crosses over Nora's face. "I did. But it didn't help." She gives me a curt nod. "You'd better go home now."

She goes inside before I can respond. I stare at her closed door for a few moments, mad at myself for not finding a way to ask her about time travel. But I think about what my aunt has just said.

Mom is like me?

19

Mom is pretty stressed out about the upcoming launch—understatement. Florida's notoriously unpredictable weather has her in a complete tizzy. She's been muttering about the rainfall coverage percentages like Troy Bridges on Channel 6 is personally out to get her.

For now, the sky is clear, but there's still plenty of time for that to change before launch time.

Meanwhile, though, Mom is thrilled that I want to go with her to work on a Saturday afternoon and that I've asked to bring some new friends with me. I'm mainly interested in the beach, which is only a short bus ride away from SpaceNow. I've already put on my swimsuit under my sundress.

"I'm so, so happy to hear you're making friends, Abby," Mom says, shoving a PowerBar into her mouth while simultaneously putting fruit and flax-seeds and spinach leaves into the blender for an another annoyingly healthy smoothie. "See what I mean? Florida's not so bad."

"Yes, it is," I say.

"Okay, okay, I give up. What are your friends like? What are their names?"

"Adam and Bix. Adam is my age; Bix is only nine." *In Earth years*, I add in my head. "But you'll like him. He's very scientifically minded."

"How did you meet them? Is Adam in one of your classes?" Mom asks.

"No, they're on vacation." I'm deliberately cryptic. "I met them at Checkers after school . . ."

"That's great," Mom says, practically giddy as she pushes the blender's *On* button.

"I like Aunt Nora," I say when the blending's done, before she has a chance to ask for more details about the boys.

"WHAT?" Mom's eyes are saucers.

"She's not that scary," I say calmly. "I only had to ring her bell five times. Then three. Do you know why all of her clocks are stopped?"

"Leave her alone, Abby." Mom pinches the top of her nose. "She's not well."

"Not well how?"

"She's a pessimist who thinks humanity is doomed."

"Well, *I* like her." I feel petulant. "But she's wrong. Humanity is not doomed."

"Exactly!" Mom looks at me, surprised. "You sound pretty certain of that."

"Oh, I'm certain," I agree. "I'm going to be fine." In my mind, I add, *Because I'm getting out of this backward century and going to live in a better one. I'll even come back for you if I feel like it. You're welcome.*

"Moving here to Florida has really changed you, Abby," Mom says, sounding smug. "For the better."

I roll my eyes and don't say anything else. Florida has not changed me at all.

But meeting a couple of time travelers has.

* * *

Adam has somehow figured out how to get his brain beacon thingy to work and interface with Merritt Island's cellular communication network. In other words, he can text my phone.

ADAM: We're outside your house. Should we come in?

Of course, locks and doorbells are probably unheard of in the twenty-third century. I rush to the door to let them in and quickly make introductions, hoping Mom won't ask too many questions. No luck there.

"So, where are your parents today? Do they want a tour too?" she asks.

"Oh, they're still on the ship," Adam says casually.

"They said we could meet up with Abby without them," Bix adds. Before she can say anything else, he does something smart—he starts asking Mom about rocket science. She bites, and they immediately begin talking in equations instead of in English. I tune them out until I hear my mom demand to know where Bix goes to school.

"I don't really go to school . . ." Bix begins.

Before I can wonder what he's going to say about his starship training program, Mom interrupts him. "Homeschool. I knew it! Do your parents—"

"Mom! Give it a rest."

"Sorry," she says, and Bix prompts her with another question about the Athena launch. I roll my eyes at Bix, who looks amused.

I turn to Adam, who looks rested in the early afternoon light. He's wearing the same light gray clothing that he's worn the past several days, but somehow it still seems clean. "Hi."

"Hey," he says back, smiling. "I like your house. It's so big!"

"Too big," I say.

To me, the house is kind of a mess. Dad is in the middle of more than one improvement project. In addition to the ripped-up bathroom, the living room is also a construction zone. I'm not even sure what he's trying to do in there—something about new flooring, I guess. I just know I'm supposed to steer clear of it for the time being.

"I miss the lower ceilings in my house back home," I add. "And our basement. And the little cozy corners and overflowing bookshelves. This place feels so empty." A lot of our stuff is still in a storage unit. Mom promised me we'd buy more furniture after her big launch. But it's more than that. Before moving here, I never gave much thought to being an only child, because it didn't really feel like I was, with my small school and practically-lifelong friendships. Here, I feel it.

"It beats my bunk," Adam says, still looking around. For the first time, I wonder if Adam likes the twenty-third century, or if he'd rather switch places with me. He'd be making a completely bananas decision if he did, and I don't like the idea of living in Avia without him, so I don't bring it up.

Adam and I sit behind Mom and Bix in Mom's compact electric car. They're talking a mile a minute in their nerd language.

I whisper to Adam, "I think chances are good that Mom will humor Bix for a few hours so we can go to the beach. Or did you really want the tour?"

"Actually, I kind of do, if it's okay with you," Adam says. "SpaceNow is in all of our history books. It would be interesting to see the beginning."

"Wow. Such a nerd."

"Well, you know what they say. Nobody's perfect."

I giggle.

* * *

Bix is asking all the right questions, which is clearly thrilling for Mom. I never asked why rockets are launched in Florida. Mom has told me anyway, of course, and now she tells Bix and Adam while she drives.

Rockets have been blasting off from Florida for more than sixty years. Back in 1960, the US government chose Cape Canaveral for early test rocket launches because it's closer to the equator than just about anywhere else in the country, and right next to the ocean. This meant that if things went kablooey (that's the technical term, trust me) after a launch and debris fell out of the sky, it wouldn't land on anyone. Also, it's better for a rocket to travel eastward, instead of westward out over the Pacific, to get an extra nudge from the Earth's spin.

Mom says it can be difficult to remember, when we're going through an Arby's drive-thru or mowing the lawn or whatever, that we are literally on a giant spinning rock in outer space. And that spinning matters for getting rockets to do their thing.

* * *

Considering that SpaceNow is the only private company ever to put a payload in Earth orbit, the first to return a spacecraft *from* low-Earth orbit, the first to deliver cargo and astronauts both to and from the International Space Station, and the first to achieve the re-flight of an orbital class rocket, you'd think its Space Coast offices would be pretty fancy, right? Wrong.

The facility is inside a sprawling industrial plant that was originally a mattress factory. SpaceNow took it over and repurposed it into a spaceport. The main building is made of white concrete and doesn't look like anything particularly special.

I've been here once before, three days after we all arrived in Florida, to see Mom's cubicle inside the Launch and Landing Control Center. Everyone has a cubicle; no one has an office. Next to all the cubicles are a factory floor, a small kitchen for the dedicated staffers who often work around the clock, and mission control. Workers gather to watch launches and recoveries, then go right back to their computers. The SpaceNow Horizontal Assembly Facility is about fifteen miles away; its landing zone is about five minutes up the coast.

After we arrive and plug in the vehicle at Mom's special parking spot, she guides us inside and occasionally stops answering Bix's steady stream of questions to point out the highlights of the facility. "At the moment, we're producing an engine a day. Before long, that'll double, then quadruple. Our rocket boosters are large robots that can actually steer themselves back home using their own internal computers."

I have to admit Mission Control does look pretty awesome. I can tell Mom notices that I'm impressed. We can't go into the Mission Control room itself, but as we peer into it from windows overhead, she turns to all three of us and launches into a little speech.

"I know we have a lot of problems, and sometimes it seems like we'll never overcome them," she begins.

We're in for it now, but Adam and Bix seem interested in what she's saying, so I don't try to interrupt her.

"The generations ahead of you kids have done a number on the environment, for one thing; we should be ashamed. But I insist you don't despair, or tune out the problems we face as human beings. Because problems *do* have solutions if we all put our minds to them. I insist that you learn all you can and become the remarkable people you're meant to become . . ."

She's going into her impassioned mode, which means she will not be deterred from speaking her mind. When she does this and Dad is around, he always crosses his eyes at me.

". . . because the days and years ahead of us are worth living for. The future will be better than the past; nothing is too good to be true. We're going to get to Mars and beyond, if I have anything to do with it, and it will happen sooner than even our leaders expect. I also think humans are going to crack the fusion threshold and fix our energy problems forever. But with or without that, we *are* figuring out how to get ourselves to other worlds. And people who can reach across space can also find ways to save nearly extinct species and feed the world's hungry millions and cure our diseases and make sure everyone's needs are met. We can find a way to give all human beings peace and a common future. Those are the days we're planning for—a time when the horizons are limitless . . ."

Mom trails off, remembering she is talking to kids, not her brilliant engineering students back home.

"Anyway, I get excited. There's a lot of energy around this place. I'm sure you kids can feel it."

I feel embarrassed by my mother, but also a little bit proud. A week ago, I probably would have faked some kind of head injury to make her stop talking, but after what I've seen through the time-sorter, I know she's actually kind of right.

I also think about what Nora said about Mom being anxious like me. Could it be true?

"You're absolutely correct, Dr. Monroe," Adam says. "We are going to do *all* of those things. Definitely."

She smiles at him. "Study hard in school. Maybe you can work here someday."

"I'd love that," Adam says. I shoot him a look and he shrugs his shoulders as if to say, *What?*

* * *

It helps to be good at math if you want to help launch and reuse rockets. Mom explained it to me a while ago, and I did actually listen. The computing challenge of launching and landing isn't that hard to explain, but it's very tough to actually perform the math in a short amount of time. And when a rocket is coming in hot, there's almost no time to make calculations.

What the spacecraft has to do is plot the best path down to a specific target on the ground without running out of fuel. NASA engineers have always known how difficult it is to land a spacecraft with any predictability, so lots of rovers and other capsules used parachutes to land—for decades. But the problem with parachutes is you can't say where they'll go. The space shuttle solved the landing problem by gliding in like an airplane. But it never traveled farther than low Earth orbit.

Which is pretty cool, but it's not, you know, *Mars*.

Anyway, to land where they're supposed to land, a rocket's computers need to solve the computation before they run out of fuel or crash into Earth—in a fraction of a second. This involves considering all the possible answers to the question of, *How can we get from here to the landing pad without running out of fuel?* and using mathematical tools to quickly choose the best way down.

From there, rockets slow a spacecraft's descent through a planet's atmosphere at hypersonic speeds. Changes in the environment can throw the rocket off course, so the onboard computers keep adjusting its trajectory to make sure it will still land within its target.

To be honest, it kind of sounds to me like rockets have an anxiety disorder—they do *a lot* of calculating and recalculating before they can come to rest.

But there's no other way.

***

We walk by an enormous laboratory. Inside, two scientists are examining small items under microscopes.

On the main factory floor, which soars more than six stories up, equipment is packed floor to ceiling, reaching all the way to the high bay LED lights. It's difficult to take it all in. Everything—from the robotic arms to the 3D printers to the clusters of horizontal Athena rockets currently in production—is white and shiny. There are a lot of places we simply can't go. Cleanliness is super important here, Mom says, because sometimes even a tiny speck of dirt can cause problems.

We walk to Mom's cubicle and Bix gets back into asking his questions. He's so smooth that she doesn't even seem to notice she's allowing him to log in to her computer, which features not one, not two, but three oversized monitors. Bix gives Adam an almost imperceptible nod, which I take to mean he's finally found enough computing power to do what he's trying to do with his oval.

"Mom, is it okay if Adam and I go to the beach now? We'll meet you back here later."

"Sure," Mom says, absorbed by whatever Bix is showing her on the middle screen. "Watch out for sharks and riptides. I mean it. Don't swim out too deep and stay near the lifeguard stand. Do you need some money? Here's a twenty."

"May I stay here with you, Dr. Monroe?" Bix asks humbly. "I've no interest in the beach, but I find your work fascinating. I promise I will remain out of the way."

"Of course," she says, not even bothering to put away proprietary SpaceNow specs as she sits down next to her new best friend. People, even smart people, always underestimate kids.

Adam grins at me: *Freedom!*

20

We walk toward the bus stop a few blocks from the SpaceNow campus. The bus will take us a few miles down the road to Cocoa Beach. Fortunately, the sun isn't quite as hot as I thought it would be. There's a breeze; it's nice as we walk.

"Your mom is intense," Adam says cheerfully.

"I know," I groan. "She drives me bananas sometimes."

"I like her," he says.

"I like her too," I say, surprising myself. "Occasionally. Even though she's always telling me to apply myself."

"And I like you," Adam adds.

"Thank you." I can't think of anything else to say that isn't awkward, so we walk in silence for a few moments. "I'm glad we're friends. I'm going to need help getting used to your time, you know. What's school like?"

Adam doesn't answer right away. "Abby, don't you think you'll miss your home? When you come with us?"

"Yes," I admit. "But when you get a chance to escape from a dystopia, you take it. That's the first rule of like every book I've ever read."

"Dystopia? This doesn't seem like a dystopia."

At this very moment, we are walking by an enormous flowering angel's trumpet plant. It's so overgrown it blocks practically all of the sidewalk. The pink flower bells are tilted up to us, toward the sun, and the air smells like a combination of flowers and sea. *Life.* Even I have to admit it doesn't feel very dystopic out today.

"I know, but that's because you can only see the surface," I say. "The world is, as you would say, kinked. That's why I'm so happy I met you guys. I see that things really do get better."

"I know there are a lot of problems here in this century, but I still don't think this is a dystopia. Is anyone listening to what we're saying right now?"

"I don't think so . . ." I admit. Although we probably are on camera.

"Are there thought police?"

"Not really . . ."

"Are you ever hungry?" he asks.

"No. But I'm luckier than a lot of people. What about the kids who don't have a nice place to live? The ones who don't feel safe where they are and can't realistically leave? The ones whose parents are in jail or the ones whose parents can't find jobs?"

What about the people, I think, *who haven't met a couple of time travelers who carry around a portal to utopia?*

"You have a big heart, Abby," Adam says quietly. "I understand what you're saying. Just because *we're* happy in this moment doesn't mean everything is okay—or safe—for everyone. Sometimes when I talk to you, I do forget to consider how much things have changed between your time and mine."

"I'm glad you understand. My mom's always saying this stuff like, 'Believe in yourself!' and 'Focus on the positive!' As if that's enough to fix what's wrong with the world right now."

"I don't know. The problems you've mentioned do get better," Adam says.

"I know! I could feel it when I touched Bix's sorter." A fresh rush of giddiness sweeps through me. "That's why I have to go to your time. All that amazing stuff probably won't happen in my lifetime, and I don't want to miss out on it. Tell me more about it. Please."

Adam thinks for a minute. "My dad always says history isn't a thing that happens apart from us, so I guess the future isn't either. We make it. I have friends on at least thirty different planets. I'm not saying we don't have problems in my time. We do. But they're very different problems than the ones your people are facing . . ."

I know I should ask Adam more about what he means, about the problems in his time, but the bus arrives, and just for a moment, I'm not in the mood to talk about problems.

It's beach time.

21

Adam and I dump all our stuff into a pile on dry sand and run out into the surf. There are people everywhere, and I'm not worried about anything for a change. Not sharks, not riptides, not sunburn, not how I look in my swimsuit. Adam whoops and begins to body surf in the small yet powerful waves. I do the same.

Over and over, the water alternately slams into us or carries us along, smooth as silk. After successfully catching a least a dozen waves, I swim to a place where I can just float, buoyed by the salt in the water, which is the perfect temperature. I almost lose track of where my body ends and the water begins. The motion of the waves is slight where I'm floating, and I give in to it completely. It reminds me of Nora's garden, the way the air melds with the water and with my flesh, the way time seems to stop for a few breaths and I no longer feel the need to act. Or even to think. I just float.

I'm hoping this is how I will always feel, once I'm in Avia.

"Do you think Bix is going to get what he needs from SpaceNow's computers?" I ask, once we're back on the sand. "What is he actually *doing*, anyway?"

Adam dries his dripping hair with one of the towels I brought. "The only way Bix can find my sister is to pinpoint where and when, exactly, she'll arrive here. You've heard of time being called the fourth dimension, right?"

"Yeah." I nod.

"Well, Bix is basically trying to do what the Athena rocket computers are trying to do when they reenter Earth's atmosphere—perform a million calculations per nanosecond to land precisely where they're supposed to land."

"I see," I say. I don't really see.

"Only he's trying to do that *and* account for an additional dimension—time. And he needed more computing power because usually the time-sorter he works with is connected to the *Audacity* when it has to perform complex tasks like this one."

"But that's impossible right now." I frown.

"Yup. Fortunately, he says the SpaceNow system is quite robust, so he can use that instead. It's a good thing we didn't show up here in 1998. Moore's Law is totally saving us."

I squint and decide to google *What is Moore's Law?* later on. "Why can't you two just let V get here, and take your time—sorry—finding her the old-fashioned way when she shows up? We could, you know, hang up posters all over the place with her picture or something. Use social media and stuff. Ask around about a girl wearing unusual clothing and describing things as 'icy.'"

"Haha," Adam says, not actually laughing. "That would probably work, but we need to find her at the exact minute she gets here, more or less, or we've got problems."

"What kind of problems? You guys have been here for days, and I don't think it's messing anything up too much. That *I've* noticed anyway. I mean, the world was plenty messed up before you got here so I don't see how you could make it worse if you tried, really."

"It's different with V. She can't stay here. Not even for five minutes."

"But why?"

Adam looks pained. "It's difficult to explain. I don't want to worry you."

"I'm not worried. For once."

"Good," Adam says. "Let's keep it that way. Things are going to work out. I can feel it. Bix has his oval; I have my intuition. We were meant to meet you and we have."

Adam smiles at me and my heart nearly stops beating. I blink, manage to smile back, and try not to blush too much. We both lean back on our arms and watch the surf.

***

The Athena rockets designed by the scientists, engineers, and computer geniuses at SpaceNow are towering examples of human ingenuity, Mom says. But they didn't appear out of nowhere. Thousands of years of experimentation and research on rockets and rocket propulsion had to happen before anyone dreamed of putting gel packs full of begonia seeds on the Red Planet.

Before we moved, I wrote a report about it and I kept it for some reason. I got an A, because Mom helped me.

The History of Rocket Science

Research by Abby Monroe
with help from Dr. Anna Monroe

(Rough draft due May 15)

One of the first machines to use the principles of
rocket flight was a wooden bird. A Greek named
Archytas built it around the year 400 BC. It was
a hollow balsa-wood pigeon suspended on wires
and propelled by escaping steam. Later on, another
Greek person named Hero of Alexandria invented
something called an aeolipile that also used steam
to move. Mr. Hero mounted a sphere on top of a
water kettle with a fire below. This turned the water
into steam, which then traveled through pipes into
the sphere. Two L-shaped tubes on each side of his
invention let the gas escape and caused it to rotate.

A few thousand miles away, the Chinese
experimented with their own tubes, only these were
filled with gunpowder. They eventually attached
bamboo tubes to arrows and launched them with
bows. Then they figured out that gunpowder tubes
could actually launch themselves. This was the
first-ever example of a true rocket made by human
beings. Martians began to plan a WELCOME
EARTHLINGS party.

In the sixteenth century, a German fireworks maker invented the step rocket, which got fireworks higher up in the sky than ever before. A big rocket carried a smaller rocket. When the large rocket burned out, the smaller one continued carrying the fireworks higher before showering the sky with embers. This design is how all rockets work today.

During the seventeenth century, Sir Isaac Newton explained his observations of physical motion in space. He wrote three scientific laws:

An object won't move by itself. Once it is in motion, it won't stop unless some force acts upon it.

When you push an object with more force it will move both faster and farther away. Also, the greater the mass of the object being moved, the greater the amount of force needed to move the object.

For every action, or motion, there is an equal and opposite reaction.

These laws of motion show exactly how rockets work—and why they are able to move in a total vacuum, which is what space is. Newton helped all the rocket scientists who came after him understand what the heck was going on.

In the twentieth century, an American named Robert Goddard began working with rockets using liquid fuel, which was challenging. These rockets had to have oxygen tanks, turbines, and combustion chambers. That's a lot of stuff, but he did it. Goddard achieved the first successful flight with a liquid-propellant rocket in 1926. His rocket flew for only two and a half seconds.

Rocket science clubs began to form in Europe in the 1930s. In Germany, one group helped develop the V-2 rocket. In 1937, German engineers and scientists got together and flew the most advanced rockets ever built. Wernher von Braun led the effort. Still, Germany lost World War II, and many unused V-2 rockets were captured by the Allies. Many German rocket scientists, including von Braun, came to the United States. Some went to the Soviet Union.

The Cold War began: The United States and the Soviet Union were the two main world powers, competing over which country was the *most* powerful. This lasted decades, and rocket science took its biggest leap forward. Both the United States and the Soviet Union saw rocketry mainly as a military weapon and poured a ton of money into developing rocket programs. In 1957, the Soviet Union launched the world's first Earth-orbiting artificial satellite,

Sputnik I. Less than a month later, the Soviets launched another satellite, this time carrying a dog named Laika on board.

A few months after that, the United States Army launched its own satellite, Explorer I. The National Aeronautics and Space Administration (NASA) was formed in 1958 with the goal of peaceful exploration of space for the benefit of all humankind. Men and women built new and bigger rockets and wrote miles and miles of computer code to accomplish amazing feats of engineering and exploration.

NASA successfully launched many people and machines into space. Astronauts orbited Earth and landed on the Moon in 1969. Robot spacecraft traveled to other planets. Satellites helped scientists to investigate remote corners of the globe, forecast the weather, and communicate instantaneously.

But space exploration has never been easy or cheap. Many brave astronauts lost their lives in the process, and budget cuts to NASA after the final moon landing in 1972 made it difficult for the United States to reach farther into space.

A Chinese American software empire founder, Madeline Wu, wanted to change that. In an interview, she said she plans to die on Mars, but not on impact. (Ha.) She founded SpaceNow in 2002. After successfully developing and flying its Athena 1 rocket, SpaceNow received funding from NASA to develop the Artemis capsule. It became the first commercial spacecraft to bring cargo to the International Space Station in 2012. To get to space, the Artemis required a heavier-lift rocket called the Athena 9, which SpaceNow first flew in 2010. Not long afterward, Wu announced a bigger rocket—the Athena Heavy—now in testing. Wu's work has had problems too, though. She has been criticized for project delays, costs that go way beyond budgets, and a colonialist attitude toward off-planet resources.

The first launch ever of the Athena Heavy is scheduled for later this year. Critics question whether space has turned into a playground or ego trip for the ultra-wealthy. SpaceNow's defenders say the launch is an important step in turning Mars into a viable option for future human settlement and in opening new doors to exploration of our solar system and beyond.

So, are rockets powered mainly by human ingenuity and hope, or by war, competition, and fear? Mom would say it depends on what you choose to focus on when you tell the story.

* * *

By the time Adam and I return to SpaceNow from the beach, Bix seems to have forgotten his main reason for being there. Instead, he and Mom appear to be doing math problems—but with letters instead of numbers—on a white board.

"This could go on for days if Bix had his way," Adam whispers to me.

"Mom, I'm hungry," I announce.

"We should get back to the ship," Adam says. "Dr. Monroe, thank you so much for allowing us to spend time with you today."

"My pleasure!" Mom beams at both boys. "We'll drive through Culver's—my treat, I insist—and then drop you both off at Port Canaveral. Would that work?"

"Perfect. Thank you again, Dr. Monroe. Bix? Does that sound good to you?"

"Does this 'Culver's' have milkshakes?" he asks.

I smile. It's the first time in days that Bix seems nine instead of, say, thirty-seven.

"Better: custard shakes!" Mom replies.

* * *

Before going to bed that night, I notice my Attractions of Florida calendar from Dad. I've been forgetting to look at it. I peel off two days and see a picture of Citrus Tower in Clermont, Florida. I read the calendar's blurb about it:

Built in 1956, the 22-story white and orange Citrus Tower in central Florida is one of the state's oldest attractions. Designed to allow visitors to observe a vista of orange groves for miles around from an indoor 360-degree observation deck, the tower is 226 feet tall and took five million pounds of concrete to build. Before Disney came to Orlando, Citrus Tower was one of the most famous landmarks and most popular attractions in the region. It is still the highest observation point in the state of Florida.

I hold my calendar in both of my hands and wonder: What is it about people? Why have we been trying to get high off the ground, by any means necessary, for so long?

22

T-MINUS 2 days TO LAUNCH

The next morning, I wake up extremely early, even before Jones and my parents. Usually when this happens, I just watch Netflix or scroll through my phone until it's time to actually get out of bed, but I don't feel like it today. Especially because so much of the local news is about the upcoming Heavy launch. News crews and spectators are starting to arrive on the Space Coast from all over the country and even the world. This launch is a significantly big deal, even to people who aren't dedicated space nerds.

But I don't need my news feed to tell me that. So I reach for the heavy old book I've been reading off and on since we got here, *Great Expectations*.

I like it for some reason. Something about the weight of its pages, its long sentences and big themes, makes me feel good . . . brainy, but in a different way than Mom. Pip, the main character, is like me. He's moving between two worlds and not particularly comfortable in either one of them. Miss Havisham and her adopted daughter Estella, whom Pip visits every week at the beginning of the story, make him nervous with their extreme wealth and deliberate cruelty. Yet he yearns to live in their world, the world of gentlemen and ladies, because he thinks it's just plain better than his own. And he does get the chance to do it. The part I'm reading now is about a secret benefactor coming forward—someone who sets Pip up with a fortune and foists him into a new universe.

"I hope you're happy, Pip," I whisper, and I try to imagine what *my* new life will be like soon.

* * *

A couple hours later, Adam and I meet up to go to the same farmer's market I visited with Juliana yesterday. This time, I decide not to bug Dad and just take my bike. It's only two miles away from my house, but I arrive sweaty. *Florida.* The sense of well-being I carried back with me from Avia is beginning to wear off.

Adam tells me Bix is pleased about what he

managed to accomplish yesterday at SpaceNow using Mom's process engineering computers, so he's planning to spend today hiding out on the boat to work on his calculations.

"I told him to try fishing instead, but he's determined to experience zero zazz—er, *enjoyment* other than sugary food during this little mission of ours," Adam tells me. "Ah well. More fun for me!"

And me, I think. Am I having fun? I am, I realize. "I'm glad you could meet up today."

Adam pushes the long swoop of his hair back from his forehead and smiles. "Me too. So, tell me again, what's a farmer's market?"

"Oh, just a place where you can buy fresh fruits and vegetables every week from the people who've grown them. Back home, we only had them in the summer and fall, but it seems like here there's one practically every day."

"Prime!"

Adam's good mood is contagious. "The Space Coast should hire you as its tourism director," I say. "You like this place more than anyone I've met who actually lives here."

"Well, if we can't return to the *Audacity*, maybe I'll get an internship," Adam says with a grin.

"Don't say that." My face falls.

"Why, Abby? Tell me again why you think you'll be happier in Avia."

I close my eyes for a moment, trying to figure out how to explain it in a new way. "Sometimes, in regular life, I feel like I'm hurting someone or something just by *existing*."

Adam widens his eyes. He looks confused; I see he's never felt this way before.

"When I take too many showers, I'm wasting water. When I throw away plastic packaging, I'm hurting the environment. When I ride on a plane, I think about glaciers breaking up thanks to all of the emissions. By buying clothes at a regular store, I might be supporting awful working conditions in a factory somewhere. I don't know for sure, but that's the kind of thing I worry about. If I get a scholarship to college someday, another kid—maybe even a more deserving one—won't get it. That feels wrong to me. I can't fix any of it and it gives me a knot in my stomach. I just want things to be better," I say. "Fairer."

"I understand," Adam says. "I do."

He grabs my hand and I feel a little bit better. I turn to him and steal a glance at his eyes, which are troubled.

"Wait, are you actually worried? About being able to get home?" I squeeze his hand so hard.

He doesn't let go of me. "Yes. But usually if you expect good things to happen, they do. So, I do."

"But what if you couldn't? What if you got stuck here?" I don't want that to happen. I don't want either of us to be stuck in this time. But I can't help wondering about worst-case scenarios.

"If Bix and V and I don't return to our own time, it isn't as if we could live the rest of our natural life spans here. Eventually—we aren't sure how long this will take—the timeline will reset to a reality in which we never existed at all. Let's not worry about that, though."

I gulp and nod.

The market is set up in the parking lot of a shopping center. There are only about twenty tents and just about everyone hands us samples, so we get to try cherry tomatoes, melon, berries, and lots of different breads and cheeses. Adam loves every morsel.

I have to admit, it's pretty nice to be able to buy food at a farmer's market whenever I feel like it. Plus these samples are delicious, and people are being so nice to us. Although it occurs to me that they might not treat everyone this way. It's weird to be reminded of the ways I'm lucky, luckier than a lot of kids.

I hear my name being yelled by a very enthusiastic voice.

"Abs! Hi!" Juliana pops up in front of Adam and me. I didn't expect to see her again today, but find that I don't mind. She's holding the hand of a little girl who is maybe five.

"Hey, Juliana. What's up? Nora liked the pastelitos. Thank you." I shade my eyes. "This is my friend Adam. Adam, Juliana. She's my . . ." I'm about to say "mentor," but realize that's a little bit weird. "She's my friend from school."

Juliana grins widely and wiggles her eyebrows at me, no doubt because Adam is extremely cute. "Super great to meet you!"

"The pleasure is mine," Adam says. They shake hands. "I'm on vacation, and Abby is showing me around. You live in such a beautiful place."

"Thank you! Yes, I think so. This is my little sister Isabel."

"Hi," Isabel says shyly. "When can I have my treat?" She pulls at Juliana's skirt.

"Soon, soon," Juliana says to her. "I gotta go. *Spectacular* meeting you, Adam. See you tomorrow, Abby!" She scoots off with a wave and calls over her shoulder, "We need to figure out when you're walking dogs with me again, okay?"

"Okay." I smile at Juliana, thinking of cute little Ruby. Once she bounces away, however, I sigh.

"What?" Adam asks.

"Oh, nothing. It's just that she's going to want to know *everything* about you tomorrow morning," I explain. "Juliana's pretty nice, but she's kind of like an investigative reporter—she'll jump all over you if she thinks you have something interesting going on. I'm still warming up to her."

"And what will you say about me?"

"Probably just that you keep following me around for some reason," I tease.

"Can't say it's not true. Let's get some snacks for Bix," he says. "He always forgets to eat. He thinks I'm unhelpful and unfocused when we get into scrapes, but I do remember the important things."

"Good idea. Hot dogs?" There's a cart near the farm stands selling foot-longs for two dollars. I still have Mom's twenty from yesterday.

"Perfect!"

We buy three hot dogs prepared Chicago-style and carefully wrapped up in two layers of paper bag. I also buy a generous container of little golden tomatoes and a nice-looking grapefruit for Dad before we walk to the marina. There's a camera high up on a pole surveying the area. I've never noticed it before. Adam follows my gaze.

"Don't worry," he says. "Bix was able to hack in to this system and loop in old footage from before we arrived. So if anyone is monitoring a screen somewhere, they won't see anything—any*one*—out of the ordinary."

"Wow, I guess you guys have it covered. Where'd you learn to do stuff like that?"

"Sometimes being stuck aboard a starship can get boring," Adam says. "You learn to amuse yourself any way you can. Bix and I have been *lots* of places we shouldn't have been."

"I see," I say, wondering what exactly he means. It's hard for me to convince Mom and Dad to let me go to a movie theater by myself, let alone get into trouble on a distant planet. I envy Adam, and I feel so much younger than him. "I wish I could say that," I admit.

Bix pops out of the boat in front of us.

"Adam, I need a small block of platinum. Then, by passing selected circuits through there"—he holds up a piece of electronic equipment I've never seen before—"as a duo-dynamic field core, I should be able to pinpoint V's arrival location."

"I brought you three hot dogs and some sun-gold tomatoes, my friend," Adam announces. "Which, I believe, is much more valuable than platinum since you have *got* to be hungry."

Bix takes a big bite of the first hot dog. He smiles for probably the first time since Culver's and devours the rest in two huge bites. I guess he likes it.

"This is an ideal level of caloric restoration, Adam. Thank you, Abby. But the problem remains: you're asking me to work with data from SpaceNow equipment, which is hardly very far ahead of a steam engine."

"Hey!" I object.

"Sorry," Bix says. "The data is a little helpful. A little," he sniffs.

"Make it work," Adam tells him firmly. "How long will it take?"

"At this rate, I might reach the first mnemonic memory circuits in three weeks, maybe a month."

"But if V will be here in six days . . ." Adam stops, noticing the dark expression on Bix's face. "Sorry. I know you're doing the best you can."

"I'm failing."

"I think," I say, "that you need a break." Bix's eyes are bloodshot. He looks like I do when I've studied too much for a test and just need to sleep.

"I am a bit tired," he admits. "I stayed up most of last night and the one before that. Perhaps a five-minute system restore is in order."

"A nap?" I ask.

"Affirmative." With that, Bix hands the precious oval to Adam, curls up on his side on the floor of the boat, and appears to fall asleep instantaneously.

"Wow," I whisper. "I wish I could do that. It takes me like an hour to fall asleep."

"Me too," Adam whispers back. "I've asked him a thousand times how he does it, and he always tells me I have to get into a habit of regular meditation."

"Ugh," I say.

"Exactly," Adam replies. We smile at each other.

"Can I please, please look at that thing again?" I gesture toward the oval. "Please? I promise I'll be careful."

Adam regards me for a few seconds, undecided. Finally he nods, almost imperceptibly. "All right. But don't tell Bix I let you."

Adam hands me the sorter.

23

When Adam hands me the oval, I feel as if he's passing me a precious infant or a priceless piece of artwork. I could not be more careful or reverent as I reach for it. When my hands make contact, I'm again transported.

This time, the scene before me is of a ship, but it's unlike any starship I've ever seen in a movie. Those are usually cold, gray, made of some kind of metal, and sterile—streamlined. This one is lush, alive. Beautiful. I stand in some kind of atrium, and the first thing I notice is all the trees. This starship is filled with organic, breathing green plants and branches thick with leaves. The ship itself seems to be made of some kind of rich wood, and each rib of its structure is hugged by undulating vines.

Again, the time-sorter begins narrating for me.

The most significant design aspect of the Audacity *is its human-friendly, tree-forward biodome. In fact, the ship itself is its own ecosystem, carefully calibrated to grow food and maintain optimal oxygen balance. People have a biological, spiritual, and psychological need to be immersed in the natural world, so this ship is designed to be an outgrowth of that world. Individuals aboard the ship can visit twelve different conservatories calibrated to match different climates on Earth. There are also two bodies of water available for swimming and other recreation.*

The largest beams of the ship are formed from genetically modified living trees. Trees not only make people feel good, they also capture pollutants in the air better than any synthetic filtration system—particulate matter, carbon monoxide, sulfur dioxide—even lead. One tree can absorb ten pounds of air pollution.

The Audacity *is home to more than twelve hundred children at any given time—including the offspring of visiting diplomats, scientists, and traders from alien planets. Kids who regularly enjoy contact with mature trees demonstrate improved memory development and better attention to their studies, in addition to deeper social interactions and overall stronger mental health.*

I begin to walk, passing people and alien beings of seemingly all ages and definitely all shapes. Each individual moves with either ease or purpose. I notice a sign for something called a Recombobulation Booth. The time-sorter senses my question and has this to say about them:

When human beings experience stress, their adrenal glands enact the fight-or-flight response. This is not optimal for interstellar travel. Thus, scientists developed a system to reduce cortisol release in the brain and quickly reduce feelings of stress. This is done by fostering the production of delta waves in the brain, similar to what the act of meditation can achieve, only much faster and with zero practice.

First used to help rehabilitate Earth's prison and jail populations, a Recombobulation Booth uses a combination of sights, sounds, smells, and even gentle pressure on key energy points on the body to quickly deliver a sensation of complete inner peace. The Booths are popular and free, as there is no system of currency or monetary exchange on any Alliance starship. Most people visit a Booth at least once per day. Some have a regimen of visiting every hour. Others prefer alternate types of immersive virtual reality experiences. It is possible to enjoy a variety of experiences in a Booth, tailored to one's unique interests.

All the adults on the ship, I see, are wearing similar fitted clothing. They almost look like they're wearing some kind of wetsuits.

Starship clothing is multipurpose, designed to offer comfort and protection from pressure changes in the environment, as well as numerous health benefits tailored to each individual wearer. Its smart technology uses timed acupressure throughout the body to relieve pain and anxiety. Its temperature regulation cools the body down when calories are consumed and promotes healing after exercise. It can deliver therapeutic warming when the wearer feels stressed or injured, and gentle vibration or weightedness to underused muscle groups to prevent atrophy in low gravity.

I'm now in a part of the ship that seems to have less gravity. I feel lighter and notice that my strides are longer. My movements require less effort. So cool.

In an area that seems designed for exercise, I see people playing games with equipment I don't immediately recognize. There's a climbing wall that works like a giant vertical treadmill, so that climbers can keep climbing without ever getting too dangerously high above the floor. Groups of humans and alien-beings do tai chi; others soak in bubbling water.

I keep walking and come upon a restaurant. Inside, robotic chefs stand before each table seating six, hibachi-style. Each robot uses knives and spatulas to guide bite-sized morsels through the air, spinning and twirling as they cook pieces of food in arcing blue flames. I watch kids take sips of their drinks not by tipping their cups toward their mouths, but by tapping out globules of liquid from little tubes and grabbing them out of the air with their tongues. Parents and older siblings roll their eyes.

I feel longing deep inside me once again. This should be my life. All the time.

24

Adam touches my elbow gently, and I know I have to give the sorter back. I do so with great reluctance, but returning from the future is easier than it was the last time.

"Thank you," Adam whispers when I hand him the precious device. "See anything good?"

"So good," I whisper back to him. "Your ship is incredible." I glance around at our current surroundings and shudder a bit at the contrast.

Bix is still napping. I wish I'd thought to hand him a pillow or a cushion. He looks so young, curled up and breathing gently.

Suddenly, he opens his eyes and sits up.

"Good morning, sunshine," I say innocently. "Feeling better?"

"My energy levels are much improved." He rubs

his eyes with one hand and reaches out with the other to take the time-sorter from Adam. "How have you two been occupying yourselves?"

"Oh, just hanging out." I don't want him to guess that I've used the sorter again, so I ask a question that has nothing to do with it. "I've been curious about something. Bix, what do you like about V? Why is she so special?"

He studies my face for a moment. I hope that he can tell from my tone that I'm not teasing him—that I genuinely want to know.

His eyes find my nose as he answers. "She never changes the subject."

"What do you mean?"

"When I'm talking about something. Even if it's esoteric or boring to other people. V never changes the subject. She just asks more questions about whatever it is I'm trying to explain."

Adam nods. "My sister is fascinated by pretty much everything. You could put her in a completely empty room with a single blade of grass and she'd be fine. She'd just learn all there is to learn about that blade. Same thing with, like, engine parts or a single droplet of water."

"She sounds unusual," I say. "And smart."

"Like popcorn, for example," Bix says. I glance at Adam and see his eyes crinkle up in something between bemusement and exasperation.

"No one in the universe is more interested in popcorn than Bix and V," Adam says.

"Try me," I say.

"Well, there are five types of corn. In our time, it's not just grown here on Earth, it's popular on many planets with Earth-like atmospheres," Bix explains. At this, I raise my eyebrows. "Only one of the five kinds pops, though. It's the variety with the hardest hull. When this type of corn is heated up, the tough shell ensures that pressure builds up as the water inside turns to steam. It's similar to a pressure cooker. The steam merges with the starch molecules and creates spongy delicious popcorn as it explodes open."

"And that," Adam interrupts, "is more than most people would want to know about it. But when Bix talked to V about this, she was all, 'Precisely how hot does it get inside the hull?' and 'How much water has to be present inside the kernel for it to pop?' and on and on."

"Indeed," Bix says. "The answers are over 300 degrees Celsius and 13.5 percent water. Approximately. I can only be precise on that value when I'm able to measure atmospheric pressure in the cooking environment."

"I see," I say. "That is definitely more information about popcorn than I've ever gotten before. All I know about it is I like kettle corn the best."

"The two of them are like that about everything," Adam says to me. "Bix follows V around spewing information, and she continuously asks for more. It's the most boring flirting you've ever seen in your life."

"It's not flirting," Bix protests again. He puts his head in his hands. "I really do miss her, though."

"Me too, buddy," Adam says. "Me too."

"We'll find her," I say.

* * *

"How was your day, kiddo?" Dad says when I get home. He's painting the bathroom, which is closer to looking normal. Mom's home too, but she's in her office on a video call.

"Not bad," I say and hand him the grapefruit I got for him at the market.

"Thanks. Looks good. Actually, can you put it in the kitchen and bring me my water bottle?"

I do as he asks and pick up a paint roller to help. Since the project is almost done, it only requires a few swipes.

"This is going to need a second coat," I observe. The color is taupe-ish and a little uneven.

"Yup. Are you volunteering?" Dad wiggles his eyebrows in the mirror at me hopefully.

"No way!"

"Well, you're off the hook for the next couple of days at least. I have to fly up to Pennsylvania tomorrow morning and tie up some loose ends at my old work."

I glance in the general direction of Mom's home office. "Is Mom okay with that?"

"She's . . . not thrilled. But she understands why I have to go." He says something about vesting stock options and *blah, blah, blah, grown-up problems*. I relax a little when he says he'll be back in two days—well before V is supposed to arrive and I'm scheduled to leave this century.

"Want to see what they're up to on *Sweetie Pies* after we get this mess cleaned up?" he asks. I nod. Most TV cooking competitions stress me out, but on this one, the stakes are so low and the contestants help each other so much that it never gets too nerve-wracking.

As I help gather up the drop cloths and rinse the paint brushes in the garage sink, I feel a stab of uncertainty. I don't want to leave my parents behind when I head to the future. There's got to be a way to bring them with me, right?

But what about my grandparents back home? What about Olivia? Jones? Can cats time travel?

What about Aunt Nora and Juliana?

Who will I miss? Who can I save?

I bite my lip, a fresh whirl of doubt spinning up inside me like a mini-tornado.

***

That night, I have a difficult time falling asleep again. It's been like a low hum in the background of my mind, the thing Nora said to me the last time I visited her: *Mom has anxiety too.* What does her tornado feel like? Why doesn't she talk about it?

In my last moments between wakefulness and sleep, I picture a long road stretching out ahead of us. Mom sees the pavement as an invitation, as something to conquer. She begins running, stopping for nothing. Her pace is sure and she pulls ahead of the rest of us, racking up miles, determined to reach some destination as fast as humanly possible. I see that she's tired, but she won't admit it.

Nora looks at the road and has a different reaction: *No, thank you.* She stops. I don't know why, but I see her there, standing still.

I'm there too, observing the road, not sure what to do. I feel uneasy and look around. I don't want to walk, so I glance up at the sky, sure there is another option—a way to find an entirely different and better path.

* * *

I wake up to a goodbye text from Dad, who's already left for the airport, and another message from the mystery number: *REFUGE.*

Before I leave for school, I look at my Florida Attractions calendar from Dad. Today it's showcasing the American Space Museum and Space Walk of Fame in Titusville, which isn't too far away from where I live now.

This museum features many items related to the history of American space exploration that have been donated by individuals, astronauts, space workers, NASA, and NASA contractor companies. Some have flown in space. It features actual Space Shuttle Launch Control Center consoles, Air Force Launch Pad 36A consoles, and a Pad 16 Launch Sequencer, as well as Mercury, Gemini, Apollo, and Shuttle monument displays in the adjacent Space View Park.

I make a mental note to tell Dad we should take Mom there for her birthday. She'll love it.

Oh, wait. I won't be here for Mom's birthday.

I push that thought out of my mind.

25

Adam texts me in homeroom. I'm super careful not to let Miss Bascom see me looking at my phone.

ADAM: We had to leave the marina.

ABBY: What? Why?

ADAM: Too many adults around. A few were giving us suspicious looks.

ABBY: Where are you?

ABBY: ???

ADAM: Don't worry.

He keeps messaging me all morning. The last text I get from him before lunch says Bix is still having trouble homing in on the exact time and place where V is likely to appear.

"You know what the problem is with chocolate-covered potato chips?" Juliana asks at lunchtime, thoughtfully holding one up between her thumb and her index finger while chewing another.

We're outside again, of course. It's ninety-four degrees. Of course.

"Hmm?" I say, distracted. I swipe through a bunch of apps, as if doing that will make a text appear.

"The problem is, they taste exactly like chocolate-covered potato chips. I mean, they're not more than the sum of their parts. Neither component is elevated by the other. It's disappointing," she says. "But then again, you can't take a single example and make an entire theory out of it. Maybe I'll have to try *dark*-chocolate-covered potato chips."

"Uh-huh," I respond.

It's been a full thirty minutes since Adam texted me. I check my phone fourteen times while Juliana and I sit together. I feel weird, like the blood has stopped flowing in my veins.

"So, are you in love, or what? I've never seen someone look at her phone that much in one ten-minute span of time. And I have two older sisters." Juliana chews. "My mom says Snapchat is the actual devil."

"I'm not *in love*," I protest. "I'm just . . . he's . . . it's hard to explain."

"He is pretty cute. So, I totally get it. Your face was *red* yesterday at the farmer's market, OMG. It was adorable."

"It was not!"

"It so was." Juliana munches her chips, apparently undeterred by their disappointing nature. "Here's my romantical advice from someone older and wiser: have fun, but don't, like, let a boy become your entire life. It's not worth it."

"I'm not doing that!"

"You are. Give me your phone," she says. "As your mentor, it's important that I step in and save you from yourself. My sister did this for me, when I got my first boyfriend in fifth grade."

"No!" I cradle the phone to my chest.

"See?" She arches a single eye brow at me, extremely pleased with herself for proving her point. The Juliana dimple is in full effect.

"Okay, okay. I'll put it away. You're worse than the teachers," I grumble, sliding my phone into my back pocket and scowling at her.

"I think it's very cute. You were all homesick and now you're lovesick. I seriously feel bad for you. You're having a rough few days."

"I'm fine," I say.

"So, is he a good kisser?" Juliana asks.

"Stop it!" I say. "I don't know if he's a good kisser or not."

"Whatever," Juliana says, grinning at me. "I bet you like Florida *now*." She crumples up her empty chip bag. "Now that you've got a man here and everything."

"I do not like Florida and I do not have a man," I say. "He's not even from here. He's on vacation."

"Well, your face is red again, so . . ."

"You are so annoying." I pull a piece of bread off my sandwich and throw it at her. I miss, even though she's only sitting like four feet away from me at the picnic table. "But thanks for taking my mind off my phone," I add weakly. "You're actually, you know, a pretty good mentor."

"I know. You're welcome."

"Hey, um, do you ever get single words and names texted to your phone from extra-long numbers?" I show Juliana the one that arrived late last night: REFUGE. "Is this, like, a Florida thing?"

"What? No, let me look at that." She grabs my phone and this time I let her. "That is *so* weird. Are you on Verizon?"

"Um, yeah. I guess I could check with them, see where these are coming from."

"You should. What the heck does 'refuge' even mean? Anyway, can you come over and walk some dogs with me after school? Just for an hour? I know you'd rather hang out with your bae but I could use the help. My mom texted me to say there were two extra check-ins today, and it's supposed to storm, so everyone's jumpy."

"Yeah, okay."

"Look at the sky," Juliana says. She tilts her head up, and I do the same. The clouds are moving fast and everything looks just a little bit yellowish. "I love storms."

26

T-MINUS 27 HOURS TO LAUNCH

By the time Juliana and I walk to the Fur Seasons after school, the air smells like rain and the wind is whipping up all the dirt and debris outside. When Juliana and I arrive, Mrs. Rivera is unhooking her hanging baskets of flowers from the entrance and bringing them inside.

"Oh good, I'm glad you girls are here. There won't be enough time before the downpour to walk the dogs, but maybe you can run them around in the yard. Then try to calm them down if you can."

Inside, we see Ruby hiding under the front desk. Juliana and I both pet her and promise to come back for her in a few minutes.

The animals at the Fur Seasons are not relaxed—not even a little. Just like on Saturday, we play with two dogs at a time, throwing their chew toys in the big fenced-in yard for them to fetch. Some do so jubilantly; some won't run around at all. They cower. We let them, knowing they sense chaos in the air.

"Let's just play with the ones who want to, and then once every dog has been outside, we'll try to comfort the scared ones," Juliana says. I nod. I admire how she knows what to do even as her hair whips around her head.

I don't want to admit it, but the weather scares me almost as much as it scares some of the dogs. Storms are different here in Florida than they are back home. They gather up steam so incredibly quickly. The sky can turn from blue to yellow to steel gray in minutes, the wind from nothing to "minor hurricane" in seconds. Same with the rain: One moment you're walking along in the sun and the next, you're completely drenched and can barely see four feet in front of you. Water seems to gush from the sky in immense bursts, not in drops. It washes away everything and makes things green and new again, but only after flooding every road, sidewalk, and yard with warm water.

It's super intense, and you definitely don't want to be outside when it happens.

This is why Dad has like four weather apps on his

phone, I realize. He's always trying to show me the radar and I'm always ignoring him.

My mind begins to race as the weather worsens: *Where are Adam and Bix? Are they safe?* If they're outside, where is the time-sorter? I try to put the questions out of my mind but I can't. I wish I could explain what's going on to Juliana because I feel like she's good at being helpful and finding solutions to problems.

There are eleven dogs staying at the Fur Seasons right now, and Juliana and I get all of them outside before the sky opens up. Once it does, the thunder and lightning are deafening and all the dogs cower in their kennels. We make sure they all have their comfort items from home, their blankets and chew toys, and we move from little partition to little partition, talking to each of the animals in low, calm voices, trying to assure them that everything will be okay. Of course, I'm not much help when I nearly jump out of my skin with every crack of thunder. I think of Olivia and how she loves storms, just like Juliana. I think about how they would like each other.

"Are you okay?" Juliana finally asks.

"Sorry. I don't enjoy storms that much," I admit.

"I can see that," Juliana says gravely. "The dogs can smell your fear. Try to take some deep breaths."

"I know, okay. Sorry." My cheeks turn pink and I feel like I'm five years old. I slow my breathing like Juliana suggests, and I feel a little bit better.

"It's fine. I'm glad you came." Juliana smiles. "Let's check on Ruby."

We walk from the kennel area back to the front, but Ruby isn't around. Mrs. Rivera is watching the local news on the computer in front of her.

"Looks like it's going to rain for a while," she says. "Do you need a ride home, Abby? It's raining too hard for you to walk."

"I do," I say. "Thank you."

She nods. "We'll take the Volkswagen. It's parked out back under the overhang, so you'll only get partially soaked."

On the drive, Mrs. Rivera asks what brought us to Merritt Island. When I tell her Mom's working for SpaceNow, she asks if Mom is excited for the launch tomorrow. It's been in the news a lot here.

"So excited," I say. "But she's under a lot of pressure right now."

What I don't say is that I kind of miss her. When Mom was working remotely, she was pretty much always home, or at this one coffee shop on our block that she was fully obsessed with. Even though she was always super busy and focused and doing like six conference calls a day, having her there in the house with me when I got back from school each day was nice. Comforting. Now, she's *rarely* home and that's kind of nice because I can do stuff like hide two boys on Dad's boat and bring them food. But it's also kind of not nice. Because it's different and different is usually worse.

"Why?" Juliana asks, snapping me back to the moment. "Why is your mom under pressure?"

I think of all the times Mom has tried to explain to me what she does and how she does it. And how even though I only ever half pay attention, I do know quite a bit about her work and about all that Space-Now is trying to accomplish on a record timeline. It's tough to figure out how much to explain to others, though. Most people like the *idea* of going to space. But when you begin to talk about the details—about what it actually takes and all the problems you actually have to solve to do it—their eyes glaze over.

Heavy-lift launch vehicles can put 44,000 to 110,000 pounds of payload into low Earth orbit and beyond, which is a lot. The Athena Heavy is the world's most powerful operational rocket, with the ability to lift 64 metric tons of weight into orbit.

That'll be useful for eventually ferrying human beings to Mars, because as soon as they get there they'll have to assemble a plant for making engine propellant. They'll also need to build a base that can support human life. To actually do this means bringing *a lot* of stuff along. The Athena Heavy is capable of putting twice as much of that stuff into orbit as the NASA space shuttles once did—and it's only the beginning. SpaceNow has plans to build an even bigger rocket next year, called the Big Athena Rocket. I've decided to nickname it the BARf—because that's what humans will do when they're in it. (Well, that's what I would do.)

The Heavy already passed its static fire test, which is where they fire up the rockets for a full ten seconds with the rocket clamped down on the launch pad. This test was the first time all of its twenty-seven rockets were "turned on" at the same time. Once the Heavy actually does blast off, all three of its nine-rocket cores will land back here on Earth for reuse. Two will come back to Cape Canaveral landing pads, one will plop itself down on a floating barge with the funny name *What Are You Still Doing Here?*

"The launch window is only ninety minutes, which is a pretty small window for such a big rocket,"

I tell Juliana and her mom. "And the Athena Heavy is the largest rocket on a launch pad since the Saturn V went up in 1973. It's a complicated thing to pull off."

"So why are they doing it?" Juliana asks. "I mean, no offense. But what's the . . ."

I can't help smiling. "The purpose?" Probably best to keep it simple. "They're putting a new space station up there. Well, part of one, anyway."

"Why?" Juliana repeats herself. "What's it gonna do out there in outer space?"

I don't point out that it's not technically going to *outer* space. Outer space is beyond our solar system, and the station isn't going that far; it'll be placed into its own orbit around the sun. "It's a lab for future scientists to use once they move beyond Earth's orbit." It all sounds kind of lonely to me, but I guess you have to plan ahead.

"Fascinating," Mrs. Rivera says.

We arrive in front of my house. I thank Juliana and her mom for the ride and run to the door as fast as I can. I see Adam and Bix there huddled under the overhang, waiting for me to let them in.

Relief washes over me even more intensely than the rainfall.

27

It's still raining, but somehow the boys haven't gotten very wet. Adam looks relaxed; Bix, agitated. I guess this is pretty much the way things always are with those two. I'm thrilled to see them, but I'm also annoyed. Adam hasn't texted me since eleven-thirty.

In other words, an eternity.

"What happened to you?" I ask, unable to keep the edge of out my voice as I enter the code in our front door keypad.

"What do you mean?" Adam is surprised at my tone. Bix rolls his eyes.

"I mean, you stopped sending me messages hours ago. I was worried."

"Oh. Sorry. I just didn't have anything new to say—"

"That's not true," Bix interrupts. "He saw your future in my sorter and it alarmed him."

"It didn't *alarm* me—"

"What?" I drop my backpack at my feet, shocked. "My future? What did you see?"

Adam shakes his head. "I didn't 'see your future.' All I saw is that you'll be *important* in the future. But don't get excited, everyone is important in the future. Even the people who lived a long time ago. I mean, how is the never to be different than the never-was?"

"Now I'm confused." My mouth goes dry.

"You are our focal point in time, Abby," Bix says. "Something happening *right now* changes our history forever. Something *you* are doing."

"But I'm not doing anything!" I protest.

"Stop it, Bix!" Adam swats at his friend, who ducks.

"What is special about you, Abby?" Bix asks. "I have to figure out what role you play in our time-line so we can make certain that events unfold as they should."

"Special about me?" I repeat. "I . . . I don't know. I'm not special, not compared to my mom. *She's* the genius, *she's* the woman on a mission. I'm just . . . around. I don't even play my clarinet anymore."

"Aw, that's not true," Adam says. "You're the iciest person we've ever met. You found us a place to stay and powerful computers and food. You're a hero, Abby."

"That's nothing," I protest. "Anyone would've done that. But I'm not special, and I don't know what I should be doing differently right now. I'm sorry."

I feel heavy. I haven't actually helped Adam and Bix all that much, and now apparently I'm messing with the timeline without even meaning to, which could mean that everyone Adam and Bix have ever loved will never even have the chance to be born.

Not to mention that I'll be stuck here forever, careening toward an immediate future that no doubt gets worse long before it gets better.

Some focal point.

My stomach hasn't been bothering me much lately, but I feel it now. It twists and gurgles, reminding me exactly what my own personal dystopia feels like. I cover my face with my hands, defeated.

Adam puts his arm around my shoulders. "Bix, try to be a little more sensitive, okay?" he says. "Abby, ignore our friend. His analytical side can be way off. I'm sure he can calculate V's arrival point without knowing exactly what impact you're having on the timeline."

Bix starts to mutter something about extra variables, but a look from Adam quiets him.

"And if you start doing anything out of the ordinary," Adam adds, "just let us know."

I almost laugh. It's not like this has been a typical week for me so far. But I nod, because I don't want Bix to think I'm holding something back.

"I'm hungry," Bix announces. "Do you have any food in there?" He points at my door.

"Yes. But be prepared to breathe in a lot of sawdust," I say, weary, letting us all in. I can't find a lost time traveler, but I *can* find us all a snack. "My dad is renovating and it's a total disaster area in here."

The downstairs bathroom is done now (except for that second coat of paint), but the living room is a mess because the new flooring hasn't arrived yet. I carefully lead Adam and Bix to the kitchen, where I pull some leftover pizza out of the fridge. While Bix attacks the food with gusto, Adam pulls me aside.

"Hey, are you okay?" he asks.

"I feel like I haven't helped enough," I answer. "I want to hold up my end of the deal."

"Yeah . . . about our deal. It's important that you understand all the risks."

I frown. "Go on."

"First of all, we don't know that much about the time vortex. It seemed fairly stable—for a vortex—when we went through it. But when we go through it from this end, it's tough to say what will happen. I don't even know if we'll be the same when we come out on the other side. We could instantly become a different age. Like four. Or thirty-seven. Or eighty-five."

"Oh." I hadn't considered that. I might like to step through and be, say, sixteen. But I'm not too sure about four or thirty-seven or eighty-five. I think of Olivia—and all that I've been longing to see again, back home. "Well, if you're willing to take that risk, I am too."

Adam takes a deep breath and holds it in for a few seconds before letting it out in a whoosh. He steals a glance at Bix, who is still eating, and then turns back to me. "There's something else you should know."

"What?"

"My sister isn't completely alone," Adam says.

"Adam . . ." Bix warns from the kitchen table, suddenly tuning in to our conversation.

"It's okay. She should know." Adam asks me, "Remember how we said V may need medical attention?"

"Oh yeah . . ." I say, not really remembering.

"There's a . . . pathogen . . . of sorts that's con-taminated my sister. Not only do we have to make sure she gets back home as quickly as possible for decontamination and treatment, we have to prevent the pathogen from spreading here in your time. If we fail, it would change everything from here on out. Bix and I will never be born."

"Wow . . ." That's all I can think to say. I look at the boys in a new way . . . with a touch of fear. Of all the worst-case scenarios I've imagined for my planet, I never would've predicted something like this.

"Yeah. We really need to get this right. And even if we do—that pathogen is widespread in our time. The future isn't perfect, Abby. It's just different."

But they have a treatment for the pathogen. V will be okay once she gets home. Because in the twenty-third century, people have it all figured out.

"I'm still going." I resist the urge to stamp my foot. There's nothing that could keep me away from Avia. It has to be better than the world I live in now. I've known that ever since I got my first glimpse of it.

Instead of replying, Adam returns to the kitchen table and grabs a slice of pizza before Bix finishes it all. He looks at me with turbulence in his bright eyes.

28

T-MINUS 20 HOURS TO LAUNCH

The past is always here, always around us. It's that ugly concrete post office building from the 1960s that looks like some kind of fallout shelter, or that calendar from 2009 that's been hanging in your garage for more than a decade, unnoticed. It's that box of toys from your childhood you just can't part with, the haircut your grandma got in 1987 and refuses to update.

Now I'm learning that the future is here too. Pressing on us, reaching back for us, pulling us toward it. Manifesting itself. All the pieces of our lives fall into place—constantly. Because the future is here. We just can't see it. Unless we're holding a time-sorter, and good luck prying one of *those* out of the extremely strong hands of a time traveler with android upgrades.

I have to figure out a new place for Adam and Bix to stay during their few remaining days in this time. The marina is out, thanks to the adults who were giving Adam and Bix the stink eye this morning. It's good they left anyway, given the wind and the rain of this afternoon. It would not have been pleasant to experience that storm in a twenty-two-foot boat. Dad will be lucky if the thing is still secure. So we need a Plan B.

I think of Nora.

I park Adam and Bix in front of our living room TV and put on an episode of *Sweetie Pies*, which they immediately love. I walk over to my aunt's property determined not to take no for an answer. She buzzes me through the front gate after only two rings. Progress.

Valentina, faithful canine servant, meets me at the door and leads me through the big house. We find Nora reading on a large chaise, upholstered in flowery fabric, in a bright and cheerful sunroom that extends off her kitchen.

"Hello, Abby," she says, setting her book down and removing her reading glasses. There are those unsettling eyes again. Valentina licks my hand and resumes her place of honor at her owner's feet. It's a very comforting scene. Serene. I feel bad for disturbing it.

"Hi, Nora." I don't know how to ask for what I need, so I crouch down to pet Valentina for a few moments. The past and the future are overwhelming. I'm glad to have a dog here to simply sit with me for a second. "I need help with something."

"I'm afraid I'm out of the problem-solving business."

"Why?"

"Haven't you ever wanted to quit anything?" She answers my question with a question.

"Yes," I say.

"Then you get it. The difference between you and me is I'm an adult who can do what she wants. It also helps to have some money in the bank. Here's some more advice, since you seem to be so interested: save your pennies, when you earn them. They come in very handy when you want to tell the world to take a long walk off a short pier."

I blink. I don't really understand Nora at all. She's unlike any adult I've ever met, and as much as I want to figure her out, she still kind of scares me. "Well . . . can I ask you for a favor? Please?"

Nora sighs. "I suppose."

"Would you let two boys—who are very nice and nerdy and a hundred percent harmless—sleep in my camping tent on your property? They're my friends and they don't have a place to stay. You can't tell my mom or dad, though."

"Where are these boys from? Why don't they have a place to stay?"

"They're from far, far away, and if I don't help them, they have nowhere to go."

Nora stares at me, hard, her golden eyes unblinking.

It begins to rain again, lightly at first, and then a deluge. We're dry inside the sunroom, but Nora gets up to close all the windows, and I help her.

"All right, your friends can camp in my garden," Nora says. "I won't say a word to anyone. You're old enough to have secrets and help people who need it."

"Thank you." I'm too relieved to say more.

Nora nods and goes back to reading her book. I text Adam.

When the rain slows to sprinkles, I let myself out. Instead of leaving, this time I wait by the gate for Adam and Bix and hold it open for them when they show up. Adam is carrying my tent, which I had him dig out of one of our new house's many closets. We choose a spot not too close to the mansion, in some good shade, to set it up. The ground is still damp, but there's nothing I can do about that.

Bix is looking around with wide eyes. "This house—it is very different from yours. If I didn't know better, I would wonder if we had traveled through time again."

"Yeah, it was built a while ago, I'm not sure how long. I like it. I *wish* my new house looked like this one."

"That's kind of you to say, Abby."

I turn around. Nora is standing between us and her aged mansion, holding a tray of food.

"Nora! I didn't think you'd come out. These are my friends Adam and Bix. Guys, this is my great-aunt, Dr. Nora Carlyle."

"Nice to meet you, gentlemen. Why don't you come in for a bit? I have snacks." She looks down at her tray and back at them. "It's still so soggy out here."

"Thank you, doctor," Adam says, giving a little bow. Bix echoes his movement; it's charming. I see Nora hiding the hint of a smile.

"You're welcome. Where are you boys from?"

"I was born on the planet—"

"Bix!" Adam gasps.

"Um. Right." This slip is so unlike Bix that Adam and I are both stunned.

Nora, on the other hand, just looks curious. "The planet . . . ? Go on."

Adam and Bix exchange a look. Bix shrugs and says, "There is a very low probability of adverse effects if we simply tell her. I checked when Abby first sent us the message to come here."

"Well, okay then," Adam says, turning to Nora. "We were both born near Tau Ceti, on Alliance starships, doctor."

"Alliance starships," Nora repeats, deadpan. "I see." She catches my eye. *Just accept it*, I try to tell her with my mind.

We all walk to the patio door and settle around Nora's kitchen counter. I see Bix look around, as if trying to find something useful. His eyes land on Nora's clocks, which are still the wrong time—the same wrong time they've been since I first visited. "Excuse me, doctor. Why aren't your clocks keeping proper time? I notice they're all set to 11:53, and they're not changing."

Nora's expression goes from open and amused to closed and dark. "Ah, that's a nod to my days at NASA," she says. "An unhappy memory I must honor."

Both boys are silent. They look to me for a cue about what to say. I'm no help. The energy in the room has shifted in a way I don't understand. We all feel it.

"Nora . . ." I begin. My instinct is to apologize, though I'm not even sure what for.

She interrupts me. "It's okay, Abby. Gentlemen, I wish you luck finding what you're looking for. Please make yourselves comfortable. Meanwhile, it's time for my afternoon siesta."

She retreats to a part of the house I've never seen and likely never will.

29

T-MINUS 8 HOURS TO LAUNCH

According to Bix's calculations, V should be arriving somewhere on Earth in the next four days or so. Our hope is that the time vortex will spit her out close to where it left Adam and Bix. While Bix is doing his endless calculations, trying to get more exact data, Adam and I decide to make the most of our remaining time in the twenty-first century. Dad's still in Pennsylvania, and Mom is of course getting ready for the launch tonight, so I cut school. Adam and I go to Checkers to get one last chocolate shake apiece. Apparently, food made from dairy isn't really a thing in the twenty-third century.

It's the most rebellious thing I've ever done, skipping school, but I don't feel guilty. My permanent record won't matter when I'm gone. I beat Adam to our meeting spot and take my worn paperback copy of *Great Expectations* out of my bag. I've almost finished the book and like it more than I thought I would. It's moody and dark—the opposite of the shiny, sunny, chain restaurant-filled world around me.

I wonder if Avia will ever have gloomy, rainy days that make me think of Pip and Estella and Miss Havisham's gothic nineteenth-century lives. I doubt it.

> ABBY: Have you ever read anything by Charles Dickens?
>
> OLIVIA: Um . . . no?
>
> ABBY: Sorry, that was random.
>
> OLIVIA: Wait! I did. I tried to, because I was so behind on my AR points last year. I started to read Oliver Twist. So depressing, I only got like eight pages in.
>
> ABBY: Oh yeah, I remember that.
>
> OLIVIA: What's going on?
>
> ABBY: I'm skipping school.
>
> OLIVIA: WHAT?
>
> ABBY: It's fine.
>
> OLIVIA: ???

Adam arrives and slides into the booth next to me. I smile at him.

ABBY: I can't really explain why right now.

OLIVIA: Are you okay?

ABBY: I'm good. <3 <3 <3

OLIVIA: ?? <3

I put my phone in my bag, vowing to send Olivia a quick video later. I may not have many more chances to communicate with her before we find V and go to Avia.

That thought feels heavy in my stomach as I go up to the counter to get some food for Adam and me.

"How did you get to be friends with Bix?" I ask when I return to our table, slurping the first sip of my extra-large shake.

"We're like brothers," Adam says fondly. "I mean, not actual brothers, but . . ."

"I get it." I nod.

"We met several years ago as cadets at Hadron camp. He was assigned as my bunkmate, and at first, I was pretty unhappy about it. Why did I have to room with some six-year-old baby? I was ten at the time and pretty full of myself. But then the kid opened his mouth, and I shut mine. He's my best friend, and the smartest, most fascinating individual I've ever known."

"You're lucky," I say. "I'm not sure who my best friend is. Before we moved, I was sure." I think of both Olivia and Juliana. "But now it feels like everything I know has been tossed up into the air, and I don't know where exactly it's going land."

"I like that," Adam says. "How you said that. I like talking to you. It's the first thing I noticed when we met, how easy it was."

I blush. "So, what is your camp training you for? What will you do when you, I don't know, graduate?"

"Hopefully, I'll be given command of a starship someday. Earth is part of a large alliance in my time, and my parents believe in trying to increase its membership in the galaxy. I believe in it too. We work to promote prosperity, peace, exploration, and science."

"That sounds beautiful," I say. "I hope you get your command. Tell me about some of the places you've been."

"Well, you know how Earth has tides? How the moon's gravity tugs at the ocean?"

"Yeah . . ."

"Well, there's this moon near Jupiter, called Io, that has no oceans. But it does have tides—tides of rock!"

"Whoa." My eyes widen. "That's awesome."

"I know!" Adam says. "Jupiter's gravity is so intense that the surface rock rises and falls every single day. There are always active volcanoes everywhere. We've never tried to land there or anything. But it's beautiful to see when you get close enough for a fly-by."

"That sounds amazing. I can't wait to see that," I say, thinking about how *stuck* we all are, at this moment, on Earth's surface. I feel a twinge, knowing how hard Mom is working as we speak to change this. Knowing what she'd think of what I'm doing now—definitely not *applying myself.*

I ask Adam where his ship is—or will be, once we find Adam's sister and return to their time.

"About . . . there," he points out the window, skyward. "You can't see it now, but it's a planet circling the far-left star in Orion's Belt."

In a few days—well, a few days and a couple of centuries—that's where I'll be. As long as we find V in time.

My phone buzzes.

MOM: Where are you? I got a call from your school.

ABBY: I didn't feel well, so I stayed home.

MOM: But you're not here!

ABBY: Um, I was. I had to run a quick errand.

MOM: You are in so much trouble right now.

ABBY: I'll be home in a few minutes.

I tell Adam I have to go and run home. Like, literally *run*. Honestly, I feel like I'm going to throw up. I've never actually gotten in trouble before. Not real trouble.

Mom meets me right at the door even though it's only two in the affternoon, and the launch is tonight, which means she should be working feverishly several miles away.

"WHERE HAVE YOU BEEN?" she demands. I can see that she's practically in tears.

"Mom, I'm fine. I just wanted to see Adam really quick," I say. "But I spent all morning in bed, for real."

"I don't believe you. I can't believe this. I had to leave work on the MOST IMPORTANT DAY IN THE COMPANY'S HISTORY. You are GROUNDED FOR A WEEK. No boys. No friends. No phone. Hand it over."

"No!" I yell. "I can't! You don't get it!"

"Oh, I get it," she says. "Hand it over right now, or it's two weeks."

I shove my phone into her hand and run for my

room, slamming the door. "All you care about is SpaceNow!" I shout at her.

"That's not true!" she yells back. "We'll discuss this later."

It's the first real fight I've ever had with Mom.

30

At the end of *Great Expectations*, Pip, the main character, goes back to Miss Havisham's estate and finds it no longer standing. It's been pulled apart and down, auctioned off years earlier, piece by piece. In a ghostly mist, Pip walks through the overgrown garden and thinks of his lost love, Estella.

As the moon rises, Pip finds Estella herself wandering through the old garden too. They talk about the past and eventually leave the ruins of the old, crumbled mansion behind, hand in hand, their pasts forever entwined with their futures, never to part again.

Miss Havisham, on the other hand, has died, full of regret for wasting her life suspended in time. A lot of people say Miss Havisham is not a realistic character, but I've been thinking about her a lot, so that's got to be worth something.

I wait until the house goes quiet. After I hear the front door slam and Mom's car pull out of the driveway, I dash over to Nora's house.

Nora mercifully lets me in on my first buzz, without an interrogation. I run to my tent, but Adam and Bix aren't there. Adam's probably still sitting at Checkers, waiting to see if I come back.

I make my way to the back patio where Nora is gardening. As soon as I see her, I burst into tears. She looks up at me, not noticeably surprised by my disheveled appearance and waterworks.

"She's impossible!" I sputter. "She moves me here for *her* dream job, not caring for one second how she's ruined my life. Then I finally meet someone I *like* and she won't let me see him! And she took my phone!"

"See who?" Nora asks, wiping her brow.

"Adam!" I spit out, as if it should be obvious. Valentina comes up to me and licks my hand. It helps, a little.

"I see," Nora says. "That does sound frustrating."

"Is that all you're going to say?"

"What do you want to hear?"

"I want to hear that you get it, that she's wrong," I say, my tears subsiding a little. I wipe my nose on my sleeve. Nora winces.

"I'm probably not going to say that, but I can tell you I felt the same way about my mother when I was your age. Let me show you something." She sets down her hoe and gestures for me to follow her.

Deeper into her garden, in a spot I'd never noticed before, is a small clearing underneath a live oak tree. From one of its mighty branches hangs a punching bag. Tucked into a cloth pocket draped over another branch at eye level is a pair of boxing gloves. Nora reaches for them and tosses them at me.

"Have a go," she says, pointing to the bag. "It helps. The worst thing you can do with your anger is nothing."

I feel self-conscious putting on the gloves, but after I take a few weak swings at the heavy bag— it doesn't move even a little—I start feeling better. I give it a few kicks too.

"I recommend some yelling," Nora says, nodding her encouragement. "I've done a lot of punching and yelling back here. Feels good."

I take a few more swings and begin to yell too. Loud, guttural sounds like I've never made before.

I don't even form words. I just yell and cry. When I look around after a few minutes, Nora isn't even there anymore. She'd returned to her gardening. But I'm not alone.

"Abby, what on Earth are you doing?" Mom steps around the tree, surveying the gardens and the beautiful house in wonder. It's the first time she's been on Nora's property.

I freeze, shocked to see her there. "I'm dealing with my anger," I say. "Not that you care. Why are you back here again? Don't they need you on the Cape?"

"I care," Mom says. "I was halfway there and I turned back around to finish our discussion. Then Aunt Nora called me to let me know you were here. Give me those gloves. I want a turn."

I take them off and toss them over gently, even though I want to throw them at her head and stomp off.

Mom has good form, and the bag even sways a little under her power. There is some real feeling behind these punches. When she turns to look at me, she has tears in her eyes.

"Look, Abby. None of this is easy for me either. Do you know how hard it is to work at a company like SpaceNow? With some of the best, smartest, most driven people in the entire country? In the entire *world*? To worry you're not going to cut it? Not even *close*? And then to find out that your precious baby daughter is cutting school to spend time with a boy you barely even know? I was terrified when I got that call from your school. Terrified." Mom isn't just teary now. She is outright crying. Sobbing. I've never seen her like this before.

"Oh," I say. I've never thought about any of it from her perspective. "I'm sorry. But you don't have to worry about Adam. And I'm not a baby."

"I know you're not," Mom says. She sits down heavily, right on the ground.

"You're worried you're not going to cut it at SpaceNow? I didn't know that," I say, sitting down too. I had no idea. I knew she was pushing herself really hard, but that was how she liked it. I thought she was living her dream. "How could you be worried? You're a genius."

She snorts. It makes her seem a lot younger than she is. "People say 'you're a genius' like it solves all problems and makes life a breeze. Trust me, it doesn't. And I'm not a genius, not by a long shot. I just work my butt off, day after day, year after year.

For what? I'm not even sure. Abby, maybe this was all a mistake. The truth is, I have no idea. You want to know the big secret of the universe? Parents don't have the answers. We don't ever get them. We're just muddling through it like everyone else. With very little help," she adds ruefully.

I stare at her. I have no idea what to say.

I feel like Mom is talking to me like we're equals, for maybe the first time . . . ever. I love it, but it also scares me. If *she* doesn't know what she's doing, we are screwed.

"I suppose that's my fault," Nora says, stepping out of the bushes. "That last part. I couldn't help but overhear."

Mom looks at the older woman and sighs, rising to her feet. "It's okay, Nora. Thank you for letting me come over to collect Abby. We'll get out of your way. I'm sorry for everything. Truly."

"Wait. I'm the one who should apologize, Anna. It's time we talked. Abby has reminded me of something important. Something I've been trying to forget about all these years."

I look back and forth between the two women, mystified.

Mom looks ready to cry again. But she doesn't.

"Abby, it's not an accident your mother is the talented scientist she is," Nora explains, looking right at me. "She comes from a long line of people who've pushed the boundaries of what was possible in math, in physics, and in all the sciences. I'm sure you know some of this."

"Yes . . ." I say, feeling sheepish. Mom is always trying to get me interested in our family history, in ancestors who were the first women in their entire towns to go to university, the first to receive a patent, the first to wear pants, et cetera. I always pretty much ignore her. Yeah, yeah, my great-grandmother went to Penn too. Pass the nachos.

"Anyway, even though your mom had lots of mentors to choose from, she picked me," Nora continues. "Me. All through your mom's childhood, I tutored her, helped her work through the hardest problems and see the toughest engineering challenges as solvable. I didn't have any children of my own, so your mother was like a daughter to me. I even paid for her go to space camp back in the eighties. Do you remember that, Anna?"

"Of course," Mom says. "Every kid in my school wanted to go to space camp. And I actually did it."

"I'd wanted to be an astronaut but ended up

being a NASA engineer instead—which was incredibly challenging, as you know, and also incredibly rewarding. But then the *Horizon* exploded," Nora sighs. "At 11:53 a.m. And something inside me broke apart, just like it did."

I remember learning about Space Shuttle *Horizon*. On its thirty-fourth mission, it collided with a tiny piece of space junk that fractured a wing. When the shuttle made its usual landing approach, the damaged shuttle's internal structure disintegrated. Space Shuttle *Horizon* broke up, killing the six astronauts on board.

"It wasn't your fault," Mom says vehemently. "You were one of the engineers who demanded the imagery of the shuttle in orbit! You knew the wing was damaged . . ."

Nora waves away what Mom is saying. "The main thing is, I didn't make myself heard."

"You have to forgive yourself," Mom says.

"Well, I couldn't. So I quit." Nora turns from Mom to me. "But I couldn't go home either. I bought this place, and I hid. From NASA, from the world, from your mother. And I'm sorry."

"Nora . . ." Mom swallows hard. "I'm sorry too. The things I said at the time . . . It scared me, to see you quitting like that. To see that quitting was an actual option, and maybe even a good one. I couldn't accept it, and the way I reacted was completely insensitive. I know that it was your decision and yours alone, and I should've respected that. Instead I made things even more painful for you. I get it now, why you had to cut off contact with me. I'm . . . not good at giving people space. Math is easy, people are . . ." She trails off. "I'm so sorry."

For a moment, no one says anything. I hold my breath, not wanting to break the spell. Finally, Nora speaks again.

"I accept your apology, Anna. And I know we should've had this talk years ago. You needed me when the going got tough, because the going *always* gets tough when you're trying to do something astonishing, and I wasn't there."

"I missed you," Mom says. She looks very small. Nora seems frozen in place, so it's up to me to hug Mom, to make her feel less alone. She clutches me like a child would. "I didn't want to let you go."

"I missed you too," Nora admits, looking stricken. "But I couldn't talk about it and I couldn't watch you throw yourself into the same field, to take all the risks I'd taken. To maybe fail as I'd failed and have your heart broken the way mine had been. All because I told you to—over and over again."

"I know," Mom sniffles. "And I understand. But I never stopped hoping we could be in each other's lives again someday. I guess that's why we're here now. I thought maybe it was time, that maybe enough years had passed—that we could talk about this stuff again."

My eyes sting. I thought my mother came here to Florida to get to space, but she came here to find her family.

To jump toward her past and bring it back to her.

We are all so lost, searching for something to grab on to.

Searching for one another.

"You were right," Nora says. "When the shuttle program was scrapped in 2011, I fell into the deepest depression of my life. We'd gone from visiting the moon when I was twenty years old to only visiting low Earth orbit when I was forty. Then, when I turned sixty, the United States couldn't even get anyone into orbit. The technology was degrading before my very eyes. I found myself not wanting to leave my house. I didn't want to see people, to look at anyone. I wasn't proud of human beings anymore."

She takes a tentative step closer to Mom and me.

"But you didn't give up, Anna. Your generation. I didn't know it at the time, exactly, but the company you're working for now was formed even before *Horizon* exploded. The seeds of the next step in human space exploration—with new materials, new computing power, new talent, new approaches— were planted, and now they're flowering. I have new hope, and it's because people like you refuse to do what I did: quit."

Another step.

"There's something about the launches—I have to see them. You get it in your bones, somehow, and I couldn't walk away—or move away, back to Penn- sylvania. I still watch every single one of them. And now there are more than ever before. I'm in awe. I'm in awe of you, Anna."

Mom smiles and looks embarrassed. "Well, it's not all me, you know. There are a few other people at SpaceNow."

"To me, it's all you. I'm sorry I disappeared."

"I'm sorry I didn't listen when you tried to tell me why."

They hug and I stare at them both with my breath held until they pull me in.

We fall apart, laughing a little and crying a little, wiping our eyes. After a few moments, it seems right to speak up: "So, how much trouble am I in if I *don't* decide to be a rocket scientist when I grow up?"

"We'll probably disown you," Nora says, crinkles forming at the edges of her inscrutable eyes.

"But for now," Mom says, "tell me more about Adam, so I can decide if you're ungrounded or not. Then I have to go."

"He's nice."

"He is," agrees Nora, winking at me. "I believe their story about where they're from. I've learned a lot."

"What? Where are they from?" Mom demands.

"It's not important," Nora says. "But I think you should unground your daughter. Those boys need her help to return home again."

"After we get the Heavy into orbit, you will tell me the rest of this story," Mom says.

"Okay," I agree.

31

T-MINUS 6 HOURS TO LAUNCH

Mom gives me my phone back and returns to the Cape. I immediately see five texts from Juliana on my lock screen. They're increasingly panicked.

JULIANA: Why aren't you in school?

JULIANA: Are you sick?

JULIANA: Abby, can you text me back? I'm at the Fur Seasons and Ruby is about to have her babies. I need your help!

JULIANA: Where are you? Text me back!!!

JULIANA: Are you ignoring me? I really need help. Ruby is in labor for real and the vet can't get here. CALL. ME.

I immediately hit the button. Juliana answers on the first ring. "What the heck, Abby?"

"I'm so sorry. My mom took away my phone. I just got all of your texts. Did Ruby have her puppies?"

"Not yet. Can you please come over?"

214

"I'll be there as quick as I can."

I hop on my bike and pedal as fast as I can. Fortunately, there's no weather this afternoon for a change and I get to the Fur Seasons in record time. I see Juliana out front, pacing with her phone. I jump off my bike and roll it right into the lobby so I don't have to lock it up. I'm breathless. "What can I do?"

"I don't know. I'm just . . . I'm freaking out. Our regular vet is on vacation and the backup vet says there's no reason for him to come but that can't be right because she's in pain and what if something's not working as it should be?" Juliana's cheeks are streaked with tears. It's hard to match the cheerful, capable, dimpled face I usually see with the one that's in front of me. "She's making sounds I've never heard her make before."

"Where's your mom?"

"She's with Ruby. We have her in her own private room in the back."

"That's good."

"I usually know how to help the animals when they're scared," Juliana says as she leads me to the back of the building, "but I've never seen puppies being born before. My family just opened this business two years ago. We came here after the hurricane."

"I didn't know you moved here because of that," I say. I look at Juliana, startled. She has suffered in ways I don't even know and never bothered to ask.

"Yeah. We had to. I miss home a lot," she says. "But I'm glad we're here. It's safer. If a big storm comes again, we can just get into the Volkswagen and drive out of its path. We couldn't do that at home."

I nod. Mrs. Rivera is in the small room with poor Ruby, who is whelping in the midst of a thick nest of multicolored blankets. The little dog is panting and shaking, but Mrs. Rivera seems calm. She's knitting.

"Hi, Abby." Her kind eyes meet my troubled ones.

"Hi, Mrs. Rivera. How's Ruby doing?"

"She's fine. She's been in the first stage here for about eight hours. Her puppies should begin arriving any moment. The vet says we should expect three."

"She's not fine, Mom. She's panting!" Juliana says.

"That's normal, mi cielito."

Mrs. Rivera catches my eye again, and I understand that Juliana is the one who needs my help, not Ruby.

"Let's give ole Rube a few minutes by herself," I suggest in the calmest voice I can muster. "Can you tell me what I missed today in social studies? I feel like I'm seriously falling behind in that class."

"I suppose," Juliana says. I can see she is torn. Her instinct to stay by her dog's side is conflicting with her wish to be a good Where Everyone Belongs mentor. I walk back to the lobby hoping she'll follow me, and she does. I see Mrs. Rivera smile a little as we retreat and feel like I've actually helped a tiny bit already.

When we get to the front, we both sit at the desk and Juliana opens her school laptop. "Why weren't you in school today? You don't look sick at all."

"I was with Adam. He's going home soon."

"WHAT? That's . . . I can't believe you skipped school, Abby. I thought you were a Good Kid."

"I *am* a Good Kid," I protest. *Am I?* I wonder.

"Good Kids don't usually skip school to hang out with their baes," Juliana says. "Especially without telling their regular friends what they're doing."

"You're right. I'm sorry. It was kind of a last-minute decision. But he's not my, um, boyfriend."

"Whatever. Okay, I wrote down all the assignments you missed today. I checked with your teachers. You're welcome."

"Thank you," I say. "I mean it."

Juliana is chewing on her lip, and I see her click away from our class portal to YouTube information about how to help dogs in labor. "I've watched, like, nine videos today and they're all terrible," she says. "They all say there's not much people can do to help dogs give birth."

"Well, that's probably the truth then, if they all say the same thing."

"I don't care! I want to do something!" Juliana cries.

"When I was here during the storm, you said I had to calm down because the dogs could smell my fear."

"Yeah."

"It's the same thing now. Ruby can smell your fear, and she needs you to be brave for her. You want to be a veterinarian, remember? On a cruise ship?"

Juliana squares her shoulders and gives me the tiniest of smiles. "You're right. That's right. Thank you. You're right."

For the first time since I made up my mind to go to the twenty-third century, I seriously waver in my decision. I feel part of something here, part of the story in this moment—at this cheerful pet resort with Juliana and Mrs. Rivera and Ruby and Ruby's painted doggy nails and her little pups getting ready to be born—in a way I haven't since I arrived.

My phone buzzes:

OLIVIA: Hey, your message before was weird. You never said why you skipped school.

ABBY: It's a long story. I'm fine, though.

OLIVIA: When can you come home for a visit? I kind of trimmed my own bangs. It's not good.

ABBY: PIC

OLIVIA: No way.

ABBY: :P

I swallow, not sure what to do next.

* * *

We hear an unusual noise from the back and look at each other in alarm. "Ruby!" Juliana cries. She tears back to the kennel and I'm right on her heels, forgetting all about Olivia's bangs.

"The first one is coming," Mrs. Rivera says. "Give her space. There's not much for us to do other than tie the umbilical cord."

We watch as Ruby strains and pushes for about ten minutes. I notice I'm holding my breath without meaning to and remind myself to try to breathe normally. I see that Juliana is practically chewing her own lip off. "Would it be okay if I played some music, Mrs. Rivera? Quietly?"

"That's a good idea, Abby. Thank you," she says. "I'm going to go get the surgical scissors and some towels."

I pull out my phone. I have no idea what to play, so I do a search for "soothing music for dogs." The first thing that comes up is a playlist called "Relax My Dog." I hit play, and something classical-sounding and sort of trippy begins. It's okay. I turn the volume down and set the phone on the floor near Ruby. The little dog doesn't seem to notice. She's hard at work.

When Mrs. Rivera returns with the towels, she hands one to Juliana and asks her to moisten it in the sink using hot water. Juliana looks at her blankly and says, "I'm not leaving," so I take the towel and do it. When I come back to the room, Juliana is sitting on the floor as close to Ruby as she can get without actually touching her.

"Here we go," Mrs. Rivera says. And she's right. A tiny puppy begins to emerge from Ruby's womb, head first. It's covered in a membrane, which Ruby instinctively begins to lick. Mother and pup look content. I see Juliana is crying, which makes me want to cry. "Happy birthday, tiny puppy," I whisper. "Welcome to Earth."

As Mrs. Rivera leaves the room to call the vet, Juliana's eyes meet mine. "She did so well," she says in disbelief. "Brave little Ruby."

"Two more to go," I remind her. "I'm never, ever having a baby. Ever."

"Me neither," my friend agrees.

We burst into giggles, breaking the tense, wondrous spell.

"What are you two laughing about?" Mrs. Rivera asks when she comes back.

"The miracle of life," Juliana replies.

"It's pretty yucky, isn't it?" Mrs. Rivera smiles. All three of us giggle until Ruby makes a sound that gets our attention. "Here comes the second puppy!"

32

T-MINUS 1 HOUR TO LAUNCH

Later, after all three puppies have been delivered safely and I'm back at the house, Adam texts that I should come over to Nora's and watch the launch on her TV.

I'm exhausted, but there's no way I'd ever say no.

Mom is, of course, back on the Cape. The big night for SpaceNow is officially here, after months and years of preparation. They are finally launching their Athena Heavy. I know I won't get into trouble, at least not bad trouble, if I go over to Nora's again.

DAD: I'm watching the launch online. Are you with Mom?

ABBY: I'm at Nora's.

DAD: Nora's? Does your Mom know you're there?

She doesn't, but I know she'd be mostly okay with it. I write back:

ABBY: The two of them had an interesting talk today. Super emo.

DAD: I heard. Can't wait to get home.

I realize that by "home," he means Florida. Weird.

When I arrive at Nora's, I find Adam reclined on the living room couch in front of the flat-screen TV, with Valentina napping nearby. I sit down next to him as CNN's cameras show us the massive rocket waiting to touch the sky. The eyes of the world are on our little neck of the woods—er, the beach.

"Where are Bix and Nora?" I ask.

"Bix talked Nora into letting him use her computer—which is actually almost as powerful as the ones at SpaceNow. He's doing some final calculations . . ."

Bix marches into the living room, holding the time-sorter in both hands. Shaking hands. "My initial prediction was incorrect," he announces. "V isn't going to arrive next week. Her arrival will be much closer to the time of the launch. I'm worried the two events will negatively impact one another."

I don't know what that means, but I'm pretty sure Bix doesn't either.

"What can we do?" Adam says, sitting up.

"All we can do is wait." Bix jumps from foot to foot.

"And watch this launch," says Nora, coming in behind him. She shoos him onto the couch, which is just big enough to fit all four of us.

Adam stands up. "I'll be back in a minute. I need some air."

He slides open one of the French doors and slips out onto the patio. I look at Bix, feeling helpless. Bix just nods at me. I decide to take that as encouragement to go after Adam.

Out on the patio, Adam has sat down on a lounge chair. He gazes at the sky, which is inching from twilight toward darkness. The ambient light of the city makes it impossible to see the stars, but he looks anyway, saying nothing. I pull another chair close to him and perch on it. I feel anxious as we wait there, together, for what humans are about to do, and for what the time vortex so many planets away from ours is hopefully about to do too. I don't know what the future holds for me, for the boys, or for anyone else. It's hard not to panic.

"What happens when V appears?" I ask. "Will Bix be able to detect it? And see where she is?"

"Yes . . . and mostly."

"How long of a window do we have to get to her before the pathogen spreads?"

"She'll probably be unconscious when she first materializes. When Bix and I came through, we were out cold for at least an hour. But even if V doesn't wake up and start wandering around, someone could see her and go up to her . . ."

"And get infected."

"Right. So we'll need to act quickly."

I feel panic rise within me as I realize I may have to leave *tonight*. I thought I had more time. If I go through with my plan to live in the future, I may not see my parents or my friends again. My breathing speeds up and I feel my heart rate rev—until I remember the voice of Avia in my mind. In Adam and Bix's incredible world, I'll be able to make things right somehow.

"Are you okay?" I ask Adam.

"I don't know," Adam answers. "I've never had anything like this happen to me before."

"Me neither," I say. "Obviously. But I'm glad it did. I mean—I'm glad we met."

"Me too," he says.

*　*　*

Minutes pass, or maybe even an hour. It feels like forever.

I hear the sound of the launch clock countdown coming from the television, loud enough to be heard through the open windows and patio doors.

"Guidance is internal and a go."

"Ignition sequence start."

Five . . .
Four . . .
Three . . .
Two . . .
One . . .

BAM.

The explosion is extremely loud. We know immediately that it doesn't look or sound the way that it should. We feel it where we sit, though we're many miles away from the launch pad.

Adam and I rush back inside. The live feed from the launch pad has cut out, and the TV talking heads are trying to explain what has gone so very wrong.

In the extreme curvature of space near a black hole, the physicist Stephen Hawking once explained, time actually does stand still. When large stars eventually collapse on themselves and form bodies so dense that not even light can escape—black holes— time comes to an end.

This moment feels like that.

***

We cry. Nora, Adam, me—even Bix. The Space-Now rocket has exploded on the launch pad. No one knows yet if the loss is partial or total.

"What does this mean for Vanessa?" Adam asks, tears streaming soundlessly down his cheeks. "What does this mean for us?"

"I . . . I don't know," Bix says, staring down at the time-sorter. "I'm not getting anything on my feeds. I can't hack around this. I just don't know."

Bix looks very small, and very young. A sob escapes from his chest and I put my arms around him, wishing I could fix things. An idea comes into my mind, and I decide to try to make him feel better—make myself feel better—in the way that V might've done if she were here. "Do you know

Polaris, Earth's North Star, is 430 light years away?" I whisper.

"Yes," Bix says, his voice wobbly. "It's a Cepheid variable, two thousand times brighter than your sun."

"Really? That's interesting," I say. Adam catches my eye and smiles the faintest of smiles. He understands what I'm doing. "What else do you know about it?" I ask.

"Polaris wasn't always your pole star," Bix begins, his voice sounding stronger and more Bix-like. "And it won't always be in the future either because the Milky Way galaxy and everything in it is constantly moving. Also, the Earth isn't steady on its axis. In thirteen thousand years, Polaris will be replaced by Vega. And sometimes Earth doesn't have a pole star at all."

"That's sad."

"It's not *sad*," Bix says. "There are other ways to navigate."

"Right," I say. "Good."

Adam shoots me a small thumbs-up.

My momentary feeling of goodness doesn't last.

I think about Mom, who has to be out of her mind with distress and disappointment, right in the middle of it all.

I send her a message:

ABBY: I saw what happened and heard it. Are you okay? I'm with Nora.

MOM: I'm okay. I'll be home as soon as I can.

ABBY: *hug*

I know she will not be home soon. The traffic during a regular launch is always gridlocked, and tonight, with all the news crews, it will be worse than ever. Like it or not, Mom will probably be sleeping at her desk, or in her car stuck on the bridge. Adam and I return to our lounge chairs on Nora's patio, and we both fall asleep like that, into our own troubled dreams.

Later, we will learn that the failure and explosion occurred because of a tiny weld defect in an engine nozzle.

Space, as they say, is hard.

33

I eventually return home and crawl into my own bed. When I wake up in the morning and go into the kitchen, it's not even 6 a.m. yet. Mom is there drinking coffee and staring at nothing. She looks terrible.

"Hi, honey. You look as sleepy as I feel," she says.

I yawn. "Can I have some coffee too?"

Mom usually discourages me from drinking her coffee (understatement), but today she nods. I pour myself some from the pot and add a lot of cream and sugar.

"I'm sorry about what happened," I say. "What now?"

"I don't know, to be honest with you," she sighs, sounding faraway. Sounding very tired. "I think maybe you were right. Maybe coming down here was all a huge mistake. I miss my students. I miss the fall leaves."

I never expected this from her. She must be even more upset than I thought. "Wait, was it a total loss? Did all twenty-seven engines burn up?"

"No, no. Just two of them. But I don't know if the actual extent of the failure matters. All those hours . . ." Mom rubs her eyes and looks around the house, which is still a mostly unfinished wreck. "I wonder how much of a hit we'd take if we put this pile of miserable stucco back on the market," she muses. "Your father will be back in a few hours; maybe we'll talk it over."

"You mean we could move back to Pennsylvania just like that?"

"We could," she says, sounding as if she's already gone. "I could get my position back, I think. We could just consider this all a bad dream. I could call the realtor right now and put it all into motion."

"Mom. Hang on. Is that really what you want?"

She sighs. "I don't know. But listen, Abby. I owe you an apology."

"Me?"

"Yes. I push too hard."

"You do push pretty hard, but I get it. You're a genius and you want me to be one too."

"What?" Mom's eyes widen. "No, that's not it at all! I'm so, so sorry. I've been . . . I . . . I think I always said all that stuff about applying yourself and being positive because I believe you're so special, so *gifted* . . . and, if I'm being honest, because I was afraid."

"Afraid of what?"

"I guess . . . afraid to just let things happen on their own without my influence or control. Afraid to admit that there's more than one way to be, to live, to feel. Afraid your empathy would only lead to depression instead of . . . Abby, I don't know. I need to trust in you. I see that now. I'm sorry."

"Oh," I say, blinking. "Um, thank you."

"You're going to have a beautiful life, but it's going to have some pain in it. I know that. It's just hard for a mama to accept. Can you understand that?"

"Are you worried I'll end up like Nora?" I ask. "Alone with a dog and a giant mansion?"

"I guess I was, a little," Mom says. "But now I see that's actually pretty great."

"Yeah, it totally is," I agree. We both laugh,

thinking of Nora's beautiful place and her awesome punching bag. "You don't have to worry about me, Mom. My stomach knot is just one part of me; it's not the whole deal."

"Oh, honey." She pulls me into a hug and we stand there like that for a long, long time.

"Okay," I say when I finally pull away. "You can worry *less*. It's not just STEM geniuses applying themselves in math classes who make the world better, you know."

"I know." Mom nods. "I do. Maybe I'll take up pottery if we move back."

"Mom . . . I think you want to stay. And I do too."

"Because of Adam?" she asks.

"No. Because of you. You're not going to quit working for SpaceNow. It's not as if the entire enterprise is going to fold up and die because of one failure."

"Meh," she says.

"Mom, you can't quit. I'm serious. Think of all the times you drove me bonkers saying stuff like, 'Every failure is just an opportunity to gather more information.' Didn't you *believe* all that stuff?"

"I half-believed it. I was trying to convince myself. And now . . . I've been working almost sixty hours a week for two years now. At some point, you've got to ask yourself, *Is it worth it?* Am I the mother I want to be? The wife?"

"Dad and I are fine," I say. "Really."

I don't know what's going to happen with Adam and Bix and the twenty-third century of my dreams, but regardless of all that, I begin to see a glimmer of future. A future in which I'll talk to Mom less as the child I've been and more as a person, stumbling along, trying to figure stuff out, together. Her relentless cheer has crumbled and it makes her seem like a human being.

It scares me—a lot—but makes me feel grown-up in a good way too.

Jones chooses this moment to saunter into the kitchen and issue a plaintive meow. I pick him up and breathe in the smell of his soft fur. He purrs, immediately contented.

"I did a lot of reading about SpaceNow before we moved, you know," I say. "Y'all have enough funding for at least three more major launches."

"Money doesn't solve everything," Mom sighs. "It doesn't solve physics. It doesn't solve politics. It doesn't solve the problem of wanting to be two different places at once."

"That's true. But what you're doing *matters*. I know you've sacrificed a ton, that you're exhausted, and that I was a total pain when we moved down here, but it's worth it. I know it is. Adam and Bix showed me a better world, a better world for everyone, and I believe it's going to come to be."

Mom nods, too choked up to say anything.

I think about my dystopia theory. I feel a shift inside, a tiny opening—the future itself reaching back to me, rearranging my perception of reality. Is trying to get to space the way to solve Earth's problems? Maybe not. But I wonder if we can do both. Would it be possible to cure diseases and feed everyone and work toward equality *and* go to space? Can we clean up the oceans, build solar farms, *and* do things that are just plain cool? Is the way forward one in which we get smaller, do less, retreat? Or is it to think bigger, get creative, improve on every front, all at once?

I don't know. But there are a lot of us, and maybe we can each pick something.

Some are creators.

Some are caretakers, healers. Teachers and helpers.

And some . . . are explorers.

"Remember President Kennedy saying, 'We do these things not because they are easy but because they are hard, because that goal will serve to organize and measure the best of our energies and skills . . .'"

I start getting choked up. I'm able to recite these words because they're from a famous world-changing speech Mom memorized and has quoted to me throughout my childhood, like a prayer, like a blessing, like a mission statement for our entire country. For our species. For our family.

She's always told me that everything worth doing in science or technology evolves because of failure. We learn more about how things work with a failure than we do with a success, at times. Strive to fail. First, calamity.

"'. . . because that challenge is one that we are willing to accept, one we are unwilling to postpone, and one which we intend to win,'" she finishes.

"You can't give up, and you can't hide. There's too much work to do. I believe in you, Mom."

She stares at me. Her cheeks are streaked with tears. My coffee is sloshed everywhere. I set down the cup.

"Wow. I'm . . . I don't know what to say. All those years, you were actually listening. Thank you, Abby. I'm . . . come here."

We hug again and cry.

"So, are you taking us to Mars, or what?"

Mom blows her nose. Her eyes are brighter now, sparkling through tears. "I think so. I really do. I feel it. But it will require people with so many diverse skill sets and perspectives working together, and the support of our whole society—not just one company or this country or that one. Maybe the answer isn't SpaceNow."

She smooths my hair and smiles at me. "I'm not sure. It feels good to admit that. There's probably more than one right way. But I still think the future *is* in space. At least part of it. And I want to help us be there."

I grin. "Aaaaaaaand she's back."

34

Mom and I are exhausted. But I don't think either one of us is that surprised when, a moment later, we hear the sound of someone leaning on a car horn outside. Mom peers out the front window and announces, "It's Nora. And she's got your friends with her."

I bolt out of my chair. "Mom, they need our help. They're looking for Adam's twin sister Vanessa, and the timing is very precise—I don't have time to explain. I have to go." My eyes plead with her to understand, to trust me.

"Okay. But I'm coming too." With that, we both go straight out the door and hop in to Nora's enormous black Escalade—Mom in the front seat, me in the back with Adam, Bix, and Valentina. I'm still wearing pajama pants and I don't even care.

"What's going on?" I demand. "Where are we going? Nora, you drive an *Escalade*?"

"Go big or go home," she says, and peels out of our driveway.

"Bix thinks he found V," Adam says. "She's here. But not as close as we'd hoped."

"My best guess is that the explosion last night veered her off course," Bix says, hurriedly thumbing his oval. "If my calculations are correct, she'll be coming out of unconsciousness shortly, on Satellite Beach. It's only fifteen minutes away if we could fly there, but with all this traffic . . ."

"Don't worry about it," Nora says. She's driving like a maniac, using the shoulder of the roads and cutting people off like there is a woman in labor in her back seat. This is a side of her I didn't expect to see, or even to exist.

"We're so grateful to you," Adam says, ever the diplomat. "Your family has saved us," he says to me in a voice barely above a whisper, and squeezes my hand.

This is it. As soon as we find V, Adam and Bix will need to take her home. One question is repeating itself over and over in my mind: When the time comes, will I stay or will I go?

Bix keeps his eyes on his screen. "They're saying only authorized personnel will be allowed on the Cape," he says.

"I'm authorized personnel," Mom says. "Good thing I grabbed my purse." She digs inside for her SpaceNow badge. We all hold our breaths as she presents it to the authorities on this side of the bridge, and let them out when they wave us through, peering curiously at the odd collection of young people—and one elderly canine—crammed into the back of the giant black SUV.

"Should be smooth sailing from here," Nora says. But she's wrong. When we reach Cape Canaveral, traffic is gridlocked.

"This is bad," Adam moans. "If V wakes up and starts wandering around, we won't be able to return home. Bix, are you getting anything? Has our ship reappeared on the timeline?"

"Not yet," Bix says. His tone is neutral but his eyes look worried.

"It's going to be okay," I say, as much to myself as to the boys. "We'll get to her, and we'll be out of here in no time. Pun intended."

Bix looks at Adam. "Are you going to let this continue? You have to tell her."

"Tell me what?"

Adam opens his mouth, but Bix speaks first "You can't come with us. It's not safe for you."

"Nothing is safe!" I snap. "We had a deal!"

"You didn't understand the terms," Adam says, not matching my volume. His voice is so quiet, in fact, that I almost don't hear it.

"Why? *Why* is it so dangerous for me to come with you?" I demand. "I know I don't understand physics, but try to explain it to me. *Try.*"

Adam closes his eyes for a moment. When he opens them, he looks older, somehow. "Abby, we haven't told you everything about where we come from," he says.

"*What is going on here?*" Mom shouts. I see Nora catch her eye in the rearview and attempt a reassuring expression. It doesn't work. Mom's eyes search mine, questioning and a little frantic.

"These two are from the future," I say, not caring whether she believes me or not. I'm focused on Adam.

"My sister isn't just our campmate," Adam begins. "She happens to be one of our very best intelligence assets and she got a little too close to the fight. She never holds anything back. Never."

My brain has only gotten as far as *Intelligence assets?* when he continues.

"That pathogen we told you about . . . it's alien. And it's our enemy."

"Huh?" I say.

"Who's V?" Mom asks.

"If you must know, she's a spy," Bix says, looking out the window. "And a critical one, at that."

"The twenty-third century isn't perfect, Abby," Adam says, rubbing the back of his neck with one hand. "I know it looks like a utopia when you see it through the time-sorter, but our Alliance is in the middle of a terrible war. A war fought without old weapons or even death—but a war even so. A war for our very souls. V is contaminated by the dorgani."

"Um, the dor-who-ey?" I repeat. I didn't sleep much last night, so it's hard to make sense of what I'm hearing.

"The dorgani are terrifying," Bix says. "Half organic, half machine. Microscopic in size; nearly impossible to combat. They've taken over close to two hundred planets in their short reign of terror so far. Once they've overcome a new planet, its technology is rendered useless and its individuals become part of a singular collective. We have decontamination treatments, but they're complicated to produce, and supply can't keep up with demand. V was close to finding a weakness in their replication system when she was . . . compromised. She had just returned to the *Audacity* for decontamination when we came within range of the vortex on Karq. Unfortunately, the space-time disruptions confused her and she jumped through the vortex before her decontamination was complete."

"We're worried," Adam adds, "that if we don't get to her quickly enough, the dorgani will spread to your society. That's why our ship only exists as a probability wave right now. If the dorgani reach you and spread, our history—your future—will be completely rewritten."

"And we'll never have been born," says Bix. "Among other significant changes, of course."

I gape at both boys. The idea of the future hanging in the balance—a future without Adam and Bix—is too much.

Nora's eyes are on the road, but I can tell she's paying very close attention to what the boys are saying. As is Mom, who—for once—is mercifully quiet.

"V needs twenty-third-century decontamination procedures, and your world needs to be protected from our enemy," Bix goes on. "If we fail, your civilization and thousands of civilizations across the galaxy are at risk of being taken over by a nearly unstoppable force—two and a half centuries before you have the tools necessary to even attempt to meet the threat."

I can't digest what I'm hearing. My brain loops back to the part about Vanessa being a spy. "But isn't V just a kid? Like us?"

"The dorgani infiltration is being fought by everyone, every day," Adam says. "It's a danger to all of us, even kids, so kids are part of the movement against it."

I don't say anything for a moment. Until I remember something. "You told me that you'd solved most of the problems we suffer from, in this time. Poverty. Energy. Inequality."

Adam nods.

"But that you had other, different problems."

Adam nods again.

"Why didn't you tell me about all this, then?" I ask. "This is kind of major." Understatement.

"I'm sorry, Abby. You were so excited about the future and I didn't want to ruin that for you, because the future *is* amazing, in a thousand different ways. But the thing is, *every* time in space has its own fight to win. We can't escape. We can't stop. We do what must be done, over and over and over again."

Mom looks at me. She's speechless. As am I.

I blink, holding back tears. I thought Adam and Bix's world was the answer. I thought it was perfect. I thought it was the end of pain. But it's not. "You never planned to take me with you, did you?" I blurt out. "You only said that so I would help you."

"We're sorry," Adam says, sounding a million years old.

"Truly," adds Bix. For the first time since I've met him, he makes eye contact with me and holds it. His dark eyes are pools of misery, of remorse.

"But without your help, Abby," Adam says, his voice low, "we wouldn't have made it this far. We owe you a debt of gratitude we can never, ever repay."

I nod, a tiny acknowledgement that they didn't mean to hurt me. They were just desperate and afraid. Like me.

I am standing at the edge of forever, and instead of seeing the utopia of my dreams, I see reality: the unfolding universe in all its unending, unyielding struggle.

35

"Hang on," Nora says and begins honking. She rolls down her tinted windows and begins yelling at the other cars to get out of her way. It works. Cars make way for us.

She gets us through in fits and starts, beyond the Cape Canaveral melee and south to Cocoa Beach. From that point on, the traffic is much lighter. Adam grasps my hand and looks into my eyes, pleading with me not to be furious about all he's said.

I don't know how to feel—but I'm not anxious for once in my life. I feel part of something huge. Something that matters—not just to me, not just to my friends, but to the world. The universe.

Nora drives well above the speed limit all the way to Satellite Beach, parking quickly and illegally in response to a yelp from Bix.

We rush across the wooden walkway that connects the street to the beach, and we all fan out. It's still very early in the morning, and the only people around are joggers and the odd metal-detector-wielding walker. I don't see anyone anywhere who could pass for a future teen spy.

"Where is she?" I shout to Adam and Bix, who are scanning the horizon fifty feet away from me.

"I don't know!" Adam shouts back, sounding panicked. I jog over to them.

"I thought she'd be here. Isn't that what the sorter says?"

"It's gone dark on me again," Bix says. "And we only have ninety minutes until our window closes on Karq."

"Failure is impossible," Adam says firmly. "What next?"

I look at Bix and his machine. Instead of glowing its normal iridescent swirl of rapidly changing colors, it's turned completely black.

The ultra-advanced time-sorter?

Bricked.

36

They say it's impossible to see the future, but that's not true, is it? Sometimes you can picture, in your mind, exactly what you have to do. You can *see* it, as clearly as if it has already occurred. It happens when you have déjà vu. It happens when you're on the tennis court in the midst of a hard-fought match and you see the winning shot before you take it, when you're playing your clarinet with the rest of the orchestra and the result of your efforts is so very much more than the sum of its parts. Flow. Wholeness. Timelessness.

Right this instant, I know exactly what I have to do.

A long time ago, like when Charles Dickens was alive, you had to use deduction to solve a mystery. You had to be good at puzzles. Very good.

Now, I realize, it's more helpful to know when to get some help from AI—or at least a search engine.

I open the Google app on my phone, which by some miracle is 87 percent charged, and type in the words I'd received from the strange number over the last month.

In a half second, this solves everything.

"I know where Adam's sister is," I announce. "We need to get back in the car. Hurry!"

* * *

The House of Refuge at Gilbert's Bar is the only remaining House of Refuge in the entire country. It's the oldest structure in Martin County and today it's a museum and sea turtle sanctuary. Originally— back in the late 1800s—there were Houses of Refuge all along the Florida coast, designed as havens for shipwrecked sailors and travelers along the sparsely populated Atlantic coastline. Before they were built, many shipwreck victims made it to the shore only to then die of starvation and thirst with no one to help them.

The Houses changed that. As part of their duties, the refuge keeper and whole family walked along the shores day after day, as far as possible, in search of shipwreck victims. When these people ended up on US soil, clinging to life, they weren't abandoned to their fate. Instead, they were given refuge. A place to recover.

The historic House of Refuge in Stuart, Florida, located in the middle of the infamous Anastasia Formation, has weathered many storms. When it was in operation, its main floor was divided into four rooms, and a wide porch surrounded the building. The north room was the kitchen. Next was the dining room, living room, and at the south end, the bedroom. All the stations were alike and all the keepers used the rooms in the same ways. The station keeper's family occupied the main floor. The attic was a dormitory for shipwrecked sailors, equipped with twenty cots with bedding and enough provisions to feed twenty men for ten days.

Now, sea turtles depend on the lifesaving measures of the House of Refuge.

Sea turtles and a time-traveling tween spy.

37

We reach Stuart in just over seventy-five minutes, thanks to Nora driving approximately ninety miles per hour. When we get to the museum and pile out of her car, it's completely quiet. It's barely seven in the morning, too early for tourists. All five of us spread out again, looking for either a way into the property or a lost-looking girl.

"Why do you think she's here?" Adam demands, stalking all over the porch.

Bix is right next to him. His time-sorter is flickering. "I have a bad feeling about this."

"I don't *think* she's here," I say. "I *know* she's here. I got a message telling me so."

"FROM WHOM?" Adam demands.

"Let's just find her," I say.

"I've got her! She's due east, fifty meters!" Bix

shouts. My heart leaps: *I'm right!*

Everyone runs toward the ocean. Valentina reaches the dark figure first, and Adam grabs her by the collar, holding her back before she can get too close.

As we catch up to the dog, I see that the person Valentina is straining toward is indeed a girl, perhaps about thirteen years old, wearing dark blue from head to toe and looking very pallid. She greets us, her twenty-first-century welcoming party, by vomiting.

"V!" Adam lets go of the dog and goes to his twin.

"Everyone else stay back!" Bix shouts.

"Sit, Valentina," calls Nora, bringing up the rear. We form a rough circle around V, keeping our distance, while Adam offers her a bottle of water. She drinks, her eyes bleary, barely open.

"The most common question . . . at this point . . . would be 'where am I?' I don't think I'll ask it," the time traveler gasps. Her voice is raspy but I see that she looks almost exactly like Adam, only with longer hair and more troubled eyes.

"Why not?" I ask.

"The answer is likely to be daunting. Old Earth? 1990? 2010?"

"Close enough," Nora says.

"We're in Florida, sis," Adam says.

"Florida?" she gasps. "I dove through one of the rarest vortices in the entire universe and ended up in *Florida*?"

Mom's eyes are wide. "Where have you come from?" she asks. Her tone is gentle.

"I am Vanessa McCain, intelligence officer in training aboard the *Audacity*. It's okay if you don't believe me. I don't believe you either."

"We believe you," I say. "We've had some time to get used to the idea."

It seems she's only been conscious for a few seconds. Adam checks her pulse and nods at Bix, who looks relieved. They've reached her in time. Still, he gestures for the rest of us to keep our distance.

And Bix's sorter appears to be working. "We're back," he says, the relief in his voice palpable.

I turn to Mom. "You doing okay?"

All she can do is sputter. "What? How?"

"Mom. You've made an entire life out of believing in impossible things, right?"

"Right . . . but . . ."

"You don't get to stop now. Trust me."

"Our ship is back online," Bix announces, looking at his oval. "What was . . . is again. Time has resumed the shape we once knew, now that we are together again and the sorter can see that V will be cured of her dorgani contamination back home. All is as it was before. Now we have to focus back to Karq and return through the vortex there to reach our time."

I go up to Adam and whisper in his ear. He nods, understanding me, and takes my hand.

"My head hurts," Vanessa says, though she's sounding stronger and looking a little less like a flu patient.

"We know, sis," says Adam. "You'll feel better soon. We're about to focus out."

V stands up shakily, leaning on Bix.

I grab Mom's hand with my free one. "There's something I need to do," I tell her, "and I need you to come with me, to help me be brave."

"Okay," Mom says. She looks terrified, which is exactly how I feel. I try not to show it.

There are no correct decisions, I realize.

You just have to deal with the ones that you make.

38

Focusing, as the time travelers call it, feels peaceful—like floating. I'm not sure if my eyes are open or closed when it's happening. I guess I don't even have eyes at all. But I do have a sense of colors and speed and time passing. It's like ten straight nights of dreaming while on cold medicine, intense and disorienting, yet somehow detached.

Rematerializing, however—that's a lot rougher. The cells of my body come together again like a car crash supernova. It's not pleasant. My essence itself flickers, neither here nor there for a few moments.

Before I know what's what, I see sharp black rocks all around me. I'm standing up, then doubled over. The air smells like sulfur and the sky above us is an odd shade of deep undulating purple. I feel strange waves of energy washing over me. It almost feels like a vibration, like a loud sound but without the sound. The ground seems to pulse, then goes still.

Adam, Bix, V, and Mom are all with me when I'm finally able to open my eyes. My mouth is dry and my ears are ringing. Adam, Bix and V appear to be fine; Mom is coughing.

"Where—where are we?" she manages to say. Or at least, I think that's what she says. My ears are still off. "How do we get back?"

"We're on the planet Karq, Dr. Monroe," Adam answers. "Don't try to move too quickly. The waves you're feeling are time dilations. The vortex is right there." He points.

About thirty meters away, there's a point between two large rocks where the air is completely still. A thin film seems to form and dissipate, form and dissipate, between the rocks. On the film are flickers of images, too faint to decipher.

It's time. I know what to do.

39

I know where my future will be, and it's not in the twenty-third century. I have to return to my own time, even though I'm right here, standing at the once-in-a-galaxy portal to a better world.

It's not because of the dorgani, either. It's because my time needs me.

There's something I need to accomplish first, though, here on Karq, next to the vortex. Something I couldn't have done without focusing here. I have to send myself a message.

Very carefully, not understanding how it will even work, I send a short text to my past self. I know it will arrive out of order and fragmented, but I also know that I will be smart enough to figure it out anyway, right when it matters the most to my friends—because I already have.

It's done. I hug Bix and Adam, waving to V since I still have to keep my distance from her contagious body. I silently will them not to lose faith in their fight. It's not necessary to speak aloud. I know they can feel what I feel and understand what I'm thinking; this place is pure energy, with no barriers or boundaries between beings. I don't have to tell them I'm not coming with them or why. I'm cloaked in love, in the wonder of this moment, the astonishing fact of our meeting in this singular place, in this singular time.

Thank you for your help, Abby, I hear Bix say in my mind. His serious face is aglow, full of intelligence and determination. My heart surges with affection for him. *Have a milkshake for me every chance you get, please. Do not worry. We will be okay.*

Better than okay. We'll make sure of it, V adds, nodding. I see no fear in her young face, only strength. *Thank you for finding me. I wish I could've stayed longer in your time. What I did see was beautiful.*

Our time is messy, Adam finishes. *But it's ours. Just as yours is yours. Do your best. Never give up. I promise I won't.* His energy is courageous and warm. It envelops me and I know we're forever connected, no matter where we go in space, in time, in the universe.

Mom is standing before the vortex, transfixed. Using gestures, she's able to slow it down and see some of the same images I saw when I got to hold Bix's sorter. I join her, peering directly into a future filled with astonishing hope and the depths of despair, astounding triumph and staggering tragedy.

Thank you for bringing me here, Mom says to me. Our minds are one, our hands are clasped. I feel alternately younger and older than her, back and forth, back and forth. It's disorienting, yet feels somehow perfectly aligned. Our energies swirl together, comfortable in the knowledge that our story on Earth is not yet fully written. Confident we will finish the job in time.

You're welcome, I reply. *I'd say 'any time,' but I think this is sort of a once-in-a-lifetime experience.*

Oh yeah. She nods, breathless. *For sure.*

Adam comes over to us. His face is glowing with the undulating purple light of the vortex, but his eyes have the same familiar glint they had on Earth. He takes both of my hands in his own, and I can somehow feel his heartbeat. I know he can feel mine as well. Tears begin running down my face, but I'm not weeping, not exactly. I'm alive with the energy of this place, with all the possibilities in time swirling before us, with new knowledge of the immense power I hold within.

Mom moves away, giving Adam and me space to say goodbye. She lightly brushes the shiny black shards of rock in our midst with her fingertips and gasps as they crumble and reform into new shapes in response to her touch.

"Remember me?" I whisper. I gaze into Adam's eyes, wishing there were some way we could stay in this moment always.

"I'll remember you forever," Adam says. He leans closer and kisses me on the cheek, hugs me for what feels like a short eternity, and whispers in my ear. I blink back new tears.

Adam nods to Bix, who tells Mom and me to prepare for focusing home.

40

Is it possible to visit a distant planet, to travel across space and time, and be the same person you were before, after it all happens?

No.

People can change in a lot of different ways, but it's hard to explain how I have. I guess it's kind of like trying to understand the moment when water heats up and goes from being a liquid to a gas. It happens gradually, then all at once, and then it's just part of the air all around us as if it were there the whole time.

Adam and Bix.

They changed my mind about so much, and I'm less worried now about whether everything is okay or not. Some days it's going to be okay, and some days it's not going to be okay. Some days it's going to be, as Adam would say, "completely kinked." All I can do is try hard to make things better, to treat others well, and to ask for help when I need it.

All I can do is never give up.

I had the chance to send a message to my past self, and when I did, I sent a message that had nothing to do with me. I sent a message that helped my friends.

I'm proud of that.

You know what's funny, though? Several days after everything happened, something made me think of my Florida Attractions calendar. I tore off a few sheets and looked at the date V arrived here. The attraction for that day?

The House of Refuge, of course.

I guess there's an easy way and a hard way to do things, and we usually choose the hard way because we don't know any better.

* * *

In the weeks after Adam, Bix, and V have returned to their not-so-utopian home century, I'm sad. But there are things that help. Juliana helps. Ruby and her new puppies help. I become a regular dog walker at the Fur Seasons, and I even sign up to be a mentor at school, to help future newbies like me find their homes here. I have a mentee from Georgia named, I'm not kidding, Georgia. I've helped her figure out how to open her locker; she's teaching me about the joys of sweet tea and manicures.

Jones helps. Nora helps. I go over to her mansion several times per month to borrow books or punch the punching bag or help rake her leaves. I think she likes me, a lot, but she won't admit it, and she keeps calling me *persistent*.

Mom doesn't bother me with positive affirmations anymore. She knows that I don't need them, that something has shifted in my bones. When you do something major, something hard, and something only *you* could've done, you don't need to be told certain things anymore. I'm glad she gets this without having to talk about it, because I can't really explain. There's a big difference between being told YOU CAN DO IT and knowing *you can do it*. Whatever *it* is.

She's back at work, and within three weeks the SpaceNow team has gotten everything fixed. A month after the failure, they have a successful launch. It's a triumph.

Dad helps. He puts me to work painting and measuring and grouting tile inside the mess that is our house-slash-construction site. You want to know what's good for twenty-first century angst? Not grouting tile. YUCK.

I begin a list about things I know about Florida in my time. Adam may not be here with me, but he's still my friend, so I'm taking his advice. I add to it as I notice things about my new home.

THINGS I KNOW ABOUT FLORIDA:

- When the magnolia trees bloom, the air smells like flowers.

- No matter how hot it gets, the mornings are perfect.

- The people here are from a lot of other places. They arrive from out of the cold, or from a distant island, or from a different country entirely, and they all want the same thing: to live a better life.

- There's no reason to be afraid of alligators or snakes. If you leave them alone, they'll leave you alone.

- There will be a time, when you're having dinner outside with your parents or with your friends, and a band is playing live music and there's a string of lights overhead and a bunch of palm trees all around you and little toddlers dancing their adorable little spin-y dances in front of the singer, and you'll think to yourself, "This isn't vacation, this is my life. This is just a Tuesday." And you'll be happy.

- Publix has very delicious bread. Their scales still don't work properly, though. That's a fact.

- The roads are very smooth. The bridges are kind of pretty. The ocean is right there, whenever you need it.

I haven't figured out my purpose yet. But for now, I'm going to pick up some garbage, google the big questions, and keep trying.

Sometimes I look up and search the night sky, knowing Adam is out there somewhere, wishing I could talk to him. Wondering if he's okay, if other future humans are okay. If we knew, right now, that billions of people in the twenty-second, twenty-third, and twenty-fourth centuries already exist, somewhere in time, how differently would we behave now to ensure they have good lives? What's our obligation to them? I'm not sure, but I do believe we have one.

I think a lot about what Adam whispered to me right before he had to go. It was this: "I'll try to get a message to you, when we get back okay," he'd said. For a long time, I thought he'd failed, that it wasn't possible.

That there was no message.

Until a day in late October when my phone started acting strange again. This time, instead of getting singular words, I just got letters. As in, an "H" or an "M." I understood right away what was going on.

Your parents probably say your phone is too expensive and that you're too addicted to it. They probably say you should put it away, participate in real life, *stop texting for one minute for the LOVE OF GOD, we're trying to have family time here.* But the next time they start in on you, maybe just tell them that your phone is capable, when the stars align, of receiving messages—very slowly—from a twenty-third-century starship. That might quiet them down for a moment or two. Or not. Parents are parents.

So, what did Adam's letters say, when I finally figured out the right order? Pretty much exactly what you'd expect them to.

ITS

GOOD

TO

BE

HOME

Questions for Discussion

1. Why does Abby's mom push her so hard and always emphasize the positive?

2. Why does Abby try to connect with Nora, even when Nora is a little unwelcoming?

3. Why does Abby want to run away to the future so badly? Why does she change her mind?

4. Adam doesn't tell Abby everything that's wrong with his time right away. Why might he have been hesitant to tell her about the bad things in the future?

5. Abby and Juliana's friendship grows over the course of the book. How does Juliana support Abby? How does Abby support Juliana?

6. Abby worries that she can't live up to her mother's high standards. She says, "I'm not special, not compared to my mom." What do you think are Abby's strengths and weaknesses?

7. Nora says that Abby and her mom, Anna, are "so much alike." How do they each respond to their anxieties about life and the future?

8. If you could grab a time-sorter to see the future like Abby, would you do it? Why or why not?

9. How does Abby's anxiety affect how she sees the world and herself? How does her relationship to her anxiety shift over the course of the story?

10. After Adam and Bix leave, Abby makes a list of things that she knows about her new home in Florida. What are some things you know and love about the place where you live? How do you feel after you make your own list?

Acknowledgments

I'd like to thank Amy Fitzgerald, Stephen Barbara, Leila Sales, Zara Friedman, Nick Penzenstadler, Anna Klenke, Jennifer Bauer, Aimee Tritt, Stuart Perelmuter, Beth McIntyre, Stacy L. Luchman, Sarah Young, Emily Golden, Tonya Ensign, Tom Bohn, Brooke Castillo, Karen Meyer, Linda Artz, Michael Schaefer, Brad Carman, and Eleanor Carman.

About the Author

Laura Schaefer is the author of *The Teashop Girls, The Secret Ingredient*, and *Littler Women: A Modern Retelling*. She is also an active coauthor or ghostwriter of several nonfiction books on personal and business development. Born and raised in Wisconsin, Laura currently lives in Windermere, Florida, with her husband and daughter, where she enjoys watching rocket launches from her front yard and visiting theme parks. Visit her online at lauraschaeferwriter.com and twitter.com/teashopgirl.